Grace
happens

by

Jan M. Czech

An Imprint of Penguin Group (USA) Inc.

acknowledgments

Special thank-yous to my agent, Steven Chudney, who gently nudged until Grace was finished and worked tirelessly to find her a home, and to my editors, Melanie Cecka and Catherine Frank. Without their wisdom Grace would never have happened.

SPEAK
Published by the Penguin Group
Penguin Group (USA) Inc., 345 Hudson Street, New York, New York 10014, U.S.A.
Penguin Group (Canada), 90 Eglinton Avenue East, Suite 700, Toronto, Ontario, Canada M4P 2Y3
(a division of Pearson Penguin Canada Inc.)
Penguin Books Ltd, 80 Strand, London WC2R 0RL, England
Penguin Ireland, 25 St Stephen's Green, Dublin 2, Ireland (a division of Penguin Books Ltd)
Penguin Group (Australia), 250 Camberwell Road, Camberwell, Victoria 3124, Australia
(a division of Pearson Australia Group Pty Ltd)
Penguin Books India Pvt Ltd, 11 Community Centre, Panchsheel Park, New Delhi - 110 017, India
Penguin Group (NZ), Cnr Airborne and Rosedale Roads, Albany, Auckland 1310, New Zealand
(a division of Pearson New Zealand Ltd)
Penguin Books (South Africa) (Pty) Ltd, 24 Sturdee Avenue, Rosebank, Johannesburg 2196, South Africa

Registered Offices: Penguin Books Ltd, 80 Strand, London WC2R 0RL, England

First published in the United States of America by Viking,
a division of Penguin Young Readers Group, 2005
Published by Speak, an imprint of Penguin Group (USA) Inc., 2007

1 3 5 7 9 10 8 6 4 2

THE LIBRARY OF CONGRESS HAS CATALOGED THE VIKING EDITION AS FOLLOWS:
Czech, Jan M.
Grace happens / by Jan M. Czech.
p. cm.
Summary: The daughter of a famous actress, fifteen-year-old Grace has never known the identity of her father, but she hopes to find some answers while spending the summer at her mother's childhood home on Martha's Vineyard.
ISBN: 0-670-05962-5 (hc)
[1. Fathers–Fiction. 2. Mothers and daughters–Fiction. 3. Secrets–Fiction.
4. Actors and actresses–Fiction. 5. Martha's Vineyard (Mass.)–Fiction.] I. Title.
PZ7.C9955Gr 2005 [Fic]–dc22 2004029924

Set in Electra
Book design by Kelley McIntyre

Puffin Books ISBN 978-0-14-240752-3

Printed in the United States of America

*To Greg, who gives me the space
and time to write and generously picks up
the slack when meals need to be cooked
and laundry piles up.*

*To Carly, who has always been
and continues to be my muse.*

To Kim, who was there when Grace was born.

Contents

1. dracula slept here

i watched the perky, blond vampire slayer drive the sharp, wooden stake through my mother's heart. Blood spurted. The body flopped and sizzled. The slayer exited stage right and, out of camera range, lit up a cigarette. I licked the pointed tip of my pencil and went back to my geometry lesson.

My name is Grace. My mother is Constance Meredith. Yeah, *that* Constance Meredith, star of stage and screen and coming soon to a multiplex near you in her latest film, *Vampire's Revenge*.

All I know is that the castle in Romania where they were shooting was cold and damp and not exactly your average math classroom. Not that I would really know what a math classroom looks like, except from television. Since Constance is always on location somewhere, I can't go to regular school. Try to imagine your teacher packing up and going with you all over the world. That's how it is with my tutor, Reginald Toffee.

Toffee is English. He was an extra in one of Constance's early movies. He played a duke or an earl or something equally British. He needed a day job and I needed a tutor. Lots of struggling actors have college degrees, and Toffee is no exception. Constance insists he's typecast as a teacher, but judging from his wardrobe, I sometimes think that he is still playing the role of British aristocracy.

Toffee is great except he loads me up with homework, and since he travels everywhere with us he makes everything a "learning experience." On this excursion I learned all I ever wanted to know about the real Dracula, a peach of a guy called Vlad the Impaler because of a nasty little habit he had of skewering his enemies' heads on stakes and planting them around the countryside.

"Actually, Grace, Vlad was the inspiration for the Bram Stoker novel *Dracula*." *Blah, blah, blah.* Toffee is full of useless information like this, but he's a good guy so I try to listen.

I had tried and failed to do the geometry proof I was working on and was about to ask Toffee for some help, when the director yelled from his perch behind the camera.

"That's a wrap. Beautiful death scene, Connie."

"Nobody calls me Connie." My mother sat up in the

coffin. Her tone of voice was cold enough to flash-freeze champagne. A stagehand scurried over. He lowered the hinged side of the fake coffin. Constance swung her legs out, took his hand, and left her tomb.

"Sorry, slip of the tongue. I was imagining opening night. The marquee spelling out CONSTANCE MEREDITH IN 'VAMPIRE'S REVENGE.'" He spread his hands as if the theater could be seen between them. "This is going to be big, babe."

"Babe?" The sarcasm in Constance's voice dripped like the phony blood on her chest. As she strode off the set to her trailer, her costume glistened scarlet in the bright lights. The heavy entrance door slammed behind her, and the director dropped his hands and scowled.

Before you get the idea that my mother is some kind of spoiled-rotten movie star who has to have everything her own way, let me tell you that you're only half right. Constance can be demanding. She can nag, hound, order, and lecture, but what mother can't? She expects a clean trailer, decent food, and use of the studio jet, but that little scene was all about respect. She has worked hard to get where she is in show business, and she deserves to be called by her given name. The given name on her official studio biography, anyhow.

"Grace, a woman in this day and age can do anything she sets her mind to, and she should do it her way. The sky is the limit." Constance told me that over and over when I was much younger and she was trying to make ends meet by waiting tables and starring in summer stock productions of *Grease*. She even bought a poster for my room that said FOLLOW YOUR DREAMS. I think it had a kitten on it. The point is that she didn't just step off the bus in L.A. and into that vampire's coffin. She worked for it and no director was going to get away with calling her Connie, a name she absolutely despised, or "babe," which she found insulting to all women.

"Oh, there will be trouble now," I whispered to Toffee. He didn't reply, but his eyes twinkled as he flicked a speck of invisible dust from his already spotless lapel.

"Big trouble. I predicted this." Camilla, my nanny, is psychic, or so she says. She has feelings about things and some of the time she's right. She always says it was fate that she met Constance in a coffee shop soon after I was born. Camilla was reading tea leaves and palms in between serving green tea and espresso. It was California. Nothing unusual about finding a psychic among the biscotti and lattes. Especially one with no last name. I asked her once why she wanted to make a living as a nanny instead of one of those psychics who works for police departments finding lost kids or even a member of a psychic friends hotline. I mean, how cool must it be to have people from all over the world call you up just to find out what's going to happen in their life? Talk about power!

"I am fulfilling my own destiny by helping Constance raise you," is all she would say about it. She can be very mysterious for someone who was born and raised in Buffalo, New York. She looks the part, too, like a gypsy straight from central casting with long, flowing skirts and waist-length curly black hair. The one thing that sometimes breaks the spell is her T-shirt collection. Everywhere we travel Camilla buys a T-shirt. I asked her why once.

"Oh Grace, I guess it's just my little rebellion. When I was your age I went to private school and had to wear a uniform. I couldn't wear jeans and T-shirts like the other kids in my neighborhood." The one she wore that night in Romania was black with a picture of the Count himself and script that read, "Vampires Are People Too."

"Nice shirt," sniffed Toffee. He wouldn't be caught dead in a T-shirt.

Something heavy crashed to the castle floor.

"Hey, be careful with that thing. We'll need it for Vamp Two," hollered the director. I watched three stagehands carry off the gilded casket my mother had "died" in. I wondered what normal kids were doing right then. Probably taking exams or going to proms or even wearing school uniforms. I knew for sure that they weren't in some dreary old castle in a country nobody had ever heard of except for its famous bloodsucker. I sighed. Normal kids would probably think it was glamorous to have my life.

But normal kids didn't have mothers who had just had a fake stake driven through their heart by a chain-smoking twenty-eight-year-old trying to play a teenager.

"I'm going to see Constance." I closed my geometry book and headed for the star's trailer.

2. frog mom

one of the things that marks an actress's rise to the top is where she changes into costume and puts on her makeup. I remember a time when Constance shared a dressing room with all the other female cast members. Talk about chaos. There were clothes everywhere and some of those girls could get pretty nasty about hogging the mirror. I've been with Constance in dressing rooms that weren't any larger than a closet, but I remember the glow on her face as she traced the painted gold star on the door. Her trailer here in Romania was state of the art—shipped in especially for her.

I raised my hand to knock when the door flew open and there was Doris, the makeup lady.

"Oh, honey, you don't want to go in there right now. Her Highness is having quite a snit."

"I think I can handle it. Thanks, Doris."

"I heard that, Doris." Constance's voice drifted out the open door. I could tell by the slight teasing tone that she had gotten over it. "Grace, come on in. We need to talk about Paris."

Constance's trailer had that new-car smell and two bedrooms. When we were on location she always tried to fix it so I could stay with her. She thought it was important that we spend time together. After years of being the star's daughter, I took these mother-daughter moments for granted. She was sitting in front of the large mirror in the bedroom she used as a dressing room, carefully removing the heavy makeup that transformed her from Constance Meredith to the Queen of the Vampires.

"Poor Doris. I didn't mean to snap at her. That little weasel of a director just made me so angry. Besides, I like to do this myself." She smiled at me in the mirror and kept working.

I smiled back and watched as the scarlet lipstick left a smear on the tissue she wiped with. The "blood" that dripped from the corner of her mouth was next, followed by the coal-black eyeliner. She popped out the cat's eye contact lenses to reveal her own hazel eyes. For about the millionth time, as I watched this process, I wondered why I hadn't inherited her striking looks. Why didn't I have the impossibly high cheekbones, the thick naturally blond hair (OK, to be honest, it was highlighted, but still . . .), the straight, aristocratic nose. My eyes were my best feature; everyone said so. I peered at them now—deep blue, almost purple. But where had they come from? Whose eyes were they? I had never met my father. Didn't even know if he was dead or alive. Constance simply refused to discuss him with me.

Whenever I asked, she said, "Who needs him? Your father was not exactly a family man, Grace. We'll discuss it when you're a little older."

With every birthday I wondered if I was old enough yet. When I was a little girl, I imagined that he had just stepped out to the store and would be right back. Later, that fantasy grew to more epic proportions. He was a spy on a very sensitive mission and couldn't live with his family because it would put us in danger. A real-life James Bond. Sometimes I suspected he was one of the actors Constance dated, and they were trying to reconcile but didn't want to tell me until it was a done deal, at which point we would all live happily ever after. In the 90210 Beverly Hills zip code, of course. I studied their handsome faces hoping to find some resemblance to my own features. By the time I was twelve, I gave up the fantasies and hoped someday to find out the reality. As I studied my face in the mirror in the depths of Romania, I was still waiting.

"Ribbit," croaked Constance. "A penny for your thoughts, Grace." Let me explain that. When I was six years old I got really mad and pitched a fit at Constance over something—nobody recalls exactly what. I yelled and hollered and said the kinds of awful things six-year-olds in the middle of tantrums say. When I ran out of "I hate yous" I finished up with "You look like a frog." I guess it was the most horrible thing I could think of to say. Constance laughed so hard I thought she was going to fall off the bed we were sitting on. Her laughter got me giggling, and soon we were rolling around the bed laughing and ribbiting at each other. That Christmas she got me a stuffed frog. I still have Froggy. It was probably one of those "you had to be there" moments, but neither of us ever forgot it.

"Ribbit. You said you wanted to talk about Paris."

"There's been a change of plans. The Paris shoot has been rescheduled."

"Don't tell me. Instead of Paris the studio has decided to finish this epic in Bora Bora. It figures I didn't pack my grass skirt." I was used to plans changing. I have been to some pretty exotic places on location with Constance. The Australian outback was cool. Toffee arranged for me to spend a day with an aboriginal tribe. In Tibet we almost got to meet the Dalai Lama. Constance owns a house in Beverly Hills and an apartment in New York. There's the ranch in Montana and the condo in Cabo San Lucas but we almost never spend more than a couple of weeks at a time in any of them, which is why what she said next really surprised me.

"You're partly right. We are going to an island. The studio is putting us on hiatus for a couple of months. Did you see Wesley trip over his own feet today trying to get out of the stunt double's way? Well, he broke his ankle. We can't shoot around him, so we have to wait until he heals." Constance squeezed the top of her nose right where it met her forehead. A sure sign she felt a migraine coming on. Personally, I was amazed my mother's costar hadn't impaled himself on one of the wooden stakes he carried for his role in this vampire epic. I've seen this guy trip over the curb climbing into a limo. He's more uncoordinated than I am, and that's really saying something. Being his stunt double is a full-time job.

"You've heard some of my friends talk about an island off the coast of Massachusetts called Martha's Vineyard, right? I thought it might be fun to spend some time there. I know a bit about the island. In fact, I lived there for a couple of years when I was in high school."

My ears perked up at this last bit of information. Constance rarely talks about her life before she hit the West Coast and began her acting career. I knew that she came from back East and that her parents were divorced. That was about all. Now, out of the blue, we were going back to a place she had once lived? Very interesting.

"Was that where my father lived, too? Who did you live with? How long are we going to stay?" I leaned forward in my chair. Constance's hand went to the top of her nose again.

"We'll be there at least a month. We'll discuss the rest of this another time. I have a horrible headache." Constance really has a way of talking about only what she wants to talk about. I have always wondered if all mothers are as evasive as she can be.

3. tripping

the next day we flew, first class of course, to Boston. I passed the time leafing through *Seventeen* magazine and the latest *Gourmet*, as well as catching up on my e-mail on my laptop. One way I try to lead a more normal life is by having pen pals. Usually I know far enough in advance where Constance will be on location, and I try to get a pen pal there. We write or e-mail back and forth to get to know each other. By the time I get to where my pen pal lives I have a ready-made friend. At least that's how it's supposed to work according to Toffee, who feels that the best way for me to learn about a place is to know someone who lives there. He contacts schools and talks to teachers and sets up the whole thing. It's safe. Not like I'm trolling the Internet or anything. Being an only child is probably lonely at times no matter where you live, but being an only child who is the daughter of a movie star who moves around as much as Constance does makes it very hard to make friends. I wondered if I would find any friends in Martha's Vineyard.

In Boston, Constance caught a flight, alone, to Martha's Vineyard.

"I want to go ahead and make sure everything is all set when you get there. Besides, there's a lot to see between here and there and I know that Toffee wants to expose you to some New England history."

"Swell, another field trip." Constance didn't reply in words. She kissed me good-bye on both cheeks. I couldn't help but notice that even after a transatlantic flight, and dressed in jeans (designer of course), a baseball cap with her hair pulled through the back, and her biggest pair of sunglasses, she was still Constance Meredith, star, a fact that didn't escape anyone as she strode down the concourse leaving a cloud of her signature perfume, C, in her wake and signing autographs as she went. The bodyguard hired by the studio to accompany her when she traveled alone was so discreet that I doubt most of the fans who approached her even noticed him.

"This sucks. Why do we have to drive?" I knew I shouldn't take my cranky mood out on Camilla and Toffee but I just couldn't help it. I dragged my feet to baggage claim and hauled my duffel bag off the carousel and into the ladies' room. A glance in the mirror sent me scrambling into my backpack for a brush, which I tried in vain to drag through my snarled hair. I gave up, splashed cold water on my face, and wondered how my mother could look so perfect.

"Someday you'll have the same knack Constance has for being low maintenance but looking high maintenance. She worked hard to learn how to always look good in public." Camilla washed her hands and fluffed out her hair.

"Are you reading my mind again?" My gaze met hers in the mirror.

"It isn't difficult to know that you're thinking, Grace. Now, let's go. Toffee is waiting."

Soon we were in the rental Jeep and on our way to a luxury hotel in Boston to sleep off our jet lag. As usual, I had trouble adjusting to the new time zone. I turned my television on, and with one eye on an infomercial that promised to erase baldness with something that resembled spray paint, I doodled on my sketch pad. After a half hour or so, my eyes felt heavy enough to let me sleep, and I put the sketch of Constance standing next to a faceless man on my bedside table.

the next morning as we drove from Boston to Woods Hole, Toffee bombarded me with facts about the American Revolution, the Salem Witch Trials, New England architecture, the Kennedys, and the Puritans and Plymouth Rock.

"Great, Toffee. Very interesting." I longed to put on my iPod and crank some tunes, but I knew that would be the height of rudeness, and I would pay for it later when Constance found out. I didn't want to spend my first week on vacation grounded.

"Pay attention, Grace. You never know when you might learn something you can use," Camilla said.

In Woods Hole we had to check in at the ferry landing. The only way to get to Martha's Vineyard is by boat or by plane.

"Will you look at the cars! How will such a small island hold so many people?" Toffee asked as he maneuvered the car into line.

The parking lot for the ferry was jammed with cars of all makes, models, and colors. Toffee pulled up behind an old rusted sedan. What the original color was I couldn't guess. It drew my eye because you never see rusted cars in Beverly Hills. I think rust is against the building codes or something. Living there is like living on another planet where the cars are always clean and everyone has perfect skin and hair. Everyone but me. Right then, a pimple was working its way out between my eyebrows just low enough so my bangs couldn't cover it.

"I have to see to the tickets. Back in a flash." Toffee

jumped out of the car and strode toward the terminal building. A few minutes later he returned waving three cans of soda dripping with condensation.

"Here you go, ladies. I swear you could prepare Chinese stir-fry on the sidewalk." He climbed into the driver's seat and the line inched forward. I chugged my soda and belched.

"Very ladylike, Grace," Camilla said. I thought about how much she sounded like a mother. Constance would have said the same thing. If she was here. Which she wasn't. After about fifteen minutes of stop-and-go movement, we drove into the bottom of the large boat.

"Let's get above decks." Toffee was already out of the car. Camilla and I followed him up the narrow stairs.

On deck, the air was cool and a brisk wind blew. Boats of all sizes and types maneuvered through the choppy water. I chose a seat near the rail, flopped down, and dug through my backpack until I found my sunglasses and iPod. Camilla opened her book, and Toffee went in search of the snack bar. I slid on my shades, adjusted the headphones of the iPod, and turned up the volume of the Rolling Stones album that I knew was next on the playlist. Mick Jagger might be old enough to be my grandfather, but I have always preferred the old bands to the new ones. It might be a side effect of growing up around adults, but I'll take Aerosmith over rap any day.

Across the deck from me, a man, woman, and two little boys ate sandwiches from a picnic basket. Their laughter reached me as the father tickled first one boy and then the other. I shifted my gaze to a teenage girl, probably about my own age, with short, spiked green hair, a miniskirt, and combat boots. She slumped against the rail and appeared to ignore the man, probably her father, who stood next to her talking nonstop. I wondered if he was divorced and this was his week with his daughter. I saw a lot of that in the movie community. Kids got passed back and forth between parents like the basketball at a Lakers game. At least I hadn't grown up like that. Maybe my father hadn't been interested enough to want me on Wednesdays, every other weekend, and for two weeks in the summer.

4. the island

i must have dozed off, because the next thing I knew Toffee was shaking my arm and motioning for me to take off my headphones.

"Grace, look. There's the island. We'll be docking in about five minutes." I looked where he was pointing and saw a ferry landing. It was as crowded as the red carpet on Oscar night. "That's the town of Oak Bluffs. The brightly colored houses you see used to be part of a church camp. They call it the campground. When people first came here they pitched tents and spent their time preaching and praying and repenting. Over time the tents became more permanent and evolved into the fancy cottages you see." Toffee was still talking, but all I heard was *Blah, blah, blah.*

I hung as far over the railing as I could and scanned

the crowd below for Constance. She hadn't said she was going to meet us, but it wouldn't be like her to avoid a crowd. Toffee went below to drive the car off.

"Let's go, Grace. Toffee will be waiting." Camilla and I fought our way from the top deck to the pier. Babies crying, people calling to friends on the landing, and the toot of the ferry's horn as the boat spit out cars from the hold made it impossible to talk. A breeze cooled my face and the smell of fried seafood made my mouth water. The blue sky dipped to meet the water, and the bustle of people brought the island alive for me. This was where Constance had lived for a while. I had never seen my mother on a bike, but as I watched the crowd, that seemed to be the most common choice of transportation. I smiled at the thought of a teenage Constance weaving in and out of traffic, perhaps turning to smile at her friends. This trip might be fun after all.

"Let's go, ladies. Constance will be at the house." Toffee was waiting in the car. We scrambled in. I put my window down and in the distance heard tinkling music. Toffee consulted the map Constance had provided him, and we were off. We wove through the narrow, crowded streets and soon found ourselves in front of one of the fancy cottages Toffee had pointed out from the ferry. Now, I've lived in some pretty unique places—the ashram in Tibet and the castle in Denmark come to mind—but this was the most normal house I'd ever seen. Porches and gingerbread trim and Chinese lanterns were everywhere. Flowers bloomed in boxes at every window. Our house in California has gates and alarm systems. Here, the front door stood wide open, protected by only an old-fashioned screen door. And on the front porch was a sight in equal parts the most normal and the most unusual of all: Constance, dressed in faded denim shorts and a tank top, her hair swept up in a crooked ponytail and her feet bare, watering a pot of geraniums on the top steps. We have gardeners and sprinkler systems. Constance doesn't water, not even house plants. Watching her accomplish this everyday task, it hit me. She had lived here. This had been her home. She had gone to school, had friends, gone on dates, and done all the things I dreamed about doing. Who had she lived here with? Her mother? Father? Both? I had never met my grandparents. They were about as real to me as Mickey Mouse. I shoved open the Jeep door and jumped out, dragging my backpack. My face felt hot; a big lump formed in my throat. My fingernails bit into my palms. Normal had always been a sort of fairy tale to me, something *other people* did. But my mother had been normal once, had known both her parents, and had lived in the same house for more than a few weeks. And, I realized it infuriated me.

"So, when were you going to tell me about this place,

Mother?" I call Constance "Mother" only when I'm really ticked off, and she knows it. She put the watering can down on the step and very deliberately faced me. Toffee and Camilla busied themselves unloading the Jeep.

"Grace, I brought us all here instead of taking hiatus somewhere else so that you could know more about what my life was like before you came into it." Constance reached a hand toward me. "Come in and I'll show you the house."

Toffee's voice rang out over the pounding in my ears. "This is private property. Leave or I'll call the authorities."

Constance and I turned just in time to see a camera flash. "Oh, I'm going to get some bucks for this picture. Constance Meredith returns to her roots." Toffee gave chase but the photographer hightailed it over a hedge and was gone. The paparazzi were nothing new in our lives.

"It's OK, Toffee. I'm not surprised. People know I'm here. It's a small island." Even through my anger I heard the tinge of resignation in my mother's voice.

I slung my backpack onto my shoulder and brushed past her and up the steps. The screen door slammed behind me and I found myself in a cool, dark foyer. The creaking door told me Constance had followed me, but I didn't turn around. The silence stretched between us like the string on a bow until I couldn't take it anymore.

"So, even the tabloids know where to find you," I

said. *"Constance Meredith comes home to roost.* Maybe they would be interested in knowing that your own daughter didn't even know where home was until yesterday." I whirled on my heel in what I thought was a pretty good Constance imitation.

"Grace, there are things you deserve to know, but you have to let me tell you in my own way. Coming here was not easy for me in many ways. I hope you can be patient with me."

For the first time that day I really saw Constance, and she looked old, ordinary. Wisps of hair fell from her messy ponytail, and dark circles ringed her eyes. Seeing her looking like a regular mother in a normal house fanned my anger. I shrugged my shoulder and the heavy backpack thudded to the floor. Constance jumped and I smirked. Apparently this wasn't going according to the script in her head.

"I think I've been plenty patient with you, Mother. Fifteen years patient." My voice rose with each syllable. I clenched and unclenched my hands. My nails dug into my palms. "How much longer do I have to wait for answers to my life? Why is that your call?"

5. family secrets

constance reached out. Her mouth moved but I blocked out her words. "Don't touch me," I hissed. She stood between me and the door, and Toffee and Camilla were outside. No escape there. I wheeled around and pounded up the stairs. I stomped into the first room I came to and slammed the door. I sank to the floor, pressed my back against the door, and let the tears come. When I was cried out, I sat with my head on my knees, listening.

The screen door creaked open and slammed shut. I heard Toffee, Camilla, and my mother in the foyer. I lifted my head and was whisked back in time. A canopy bed with lacy throw pillows, a dressing table with a floral skirt that matched the bedspread and curtains, and a night table with a pink phone greeted me. A white bureau trimmed in gold stood between two long windows. My head pounded.

I stood up slowly and caught my reflection in the dressing table mirror. Eyes puffed into slits, red nose, flat hair. *Lovely*. The anger had rolled out of me with my tears. I felt hollow as a pumpkin the day after Halloween. I knew from experience that after one of my tantrums no one would bother me for a while. I don't remember which shrink gave Constance the advice to respect my space after an outburst, but she took it to heart. I flung myself onto the bed, scattering lacy pillows to the floor, closed my eyes, and dozed off.

When I woke up the pounding in my head had been replaced by a tapping on the door.

"Come in." I sat up as Constance opened the door and stuck her head into the room.

"Are you feeling better, Gracie? I was hoping we could talk." She raised her eyebrows and the corners of her mouth lifted in a halfhearted smile.

I swung my legs over the side of the bed and met her eyes. Constance took a step into the room. "You might have guessed this is my old room," she said. "How about I show you the rest of the house and I'll have Toffee bring up your bags? You can unpack later."

"OK, let's start with a house tour." I decided I might as well take what I could get for the time being. Constance smiled and tucked a strand of hair behind her right ear.

"Well then, let's get to it." She led the way down the

stairs into the small foyer. "You'll see this is actually a very small house, more of a cottage really. We have the living room, study and kitchen off the foyer here and three bedrooms and a bath upstairs. With you in my old room, I'll take my father's room, Camilla can have the guest room, and Toffee will bunk in the study."

"Your father's room?" A small flame of anger warmed my face and I struggled to keep my voice even. Losing control now wouldn't get me anywhere. "You've never really talked about your parents except to say they didn't get along. Did you live here with him?" We moved across the foyer into the small living room. Sunlight filtered through the lace curtains and onto some mismatched wicker furniture arranged on a faded Oriental rug.

I sank into a rocking chair and idly pushed my foot against the floor to get the chair moving. The room was spotless. Someone had kept this place clean and planted the flowers. Someone that Constance had arranged for like she arranged for the help at all our other houses. Except our other houses weren't kept secret from me.

Constance sat cross-legged on the couch across from me. She studied her fingernails, then turned her hands palm-up then palm-down. Silence stretched between us like a rubber band. I had never seen my mother fidget. She was always in charge, always presenting a totally together face to her audience. Finally, she sighed and looked up. "I lived here for two years with my father, from the time I was sixteen until I graduated from high school. These houses in the campgrounds are usually passed down through families, and this one was my grandparents'. I used to come here when I was a little girl. Sometimes I spent the entire summer here while my father traveled around on construction jobs. When my grandparents died, the house came to him and we moved here. There was a lot of building going on here and he was able to find plenty of work."

"But where was your mother?" I was wrapping my mind around the fact that maybe Constance hadn't had all that normal a childhood after all.

"I told you my parents didn't get along, but there was more than that. My mother left us, my father and me, when I was five years old. She decided she didn't want a child to raise, and the moving around we did wasn't to her liking. She wanted a regular life, a regular house, and to answer to nobody but herself. It seemed to me that she fell out of love with us. My father raised me as well as he could." Tears glistened in the corners of her eyes.

"Like you're trying to do with me?" If Constance heard the sarcasm in my voice, she chose to ignore it.

"Yes, Grace. I'm doing my best even though I know you don't always think so." She wiped her eyes with the back of her hand.

"So, when he died, the house came to you? You hired people to take care of it?" I thought I had this part of Constance's story figured out, but I was wrong.

"Grace, my father isn't dead." Constance's eyes never left mine. She didn't blink. I felt like a baseball was stuck in my throat. My stomach rolled and flipped and my face flamed.

"You're telling me I have a grandfather I've never met?" My voice grew shriller with every word, but I couldn't help it. Family. I had family besides the father who had been kept from me. I had a grandfather I could have spent summers with here in this house. Normal summers going to the beach, hanging out in my room, and having friends instead of touring the grand old cities of Europe or jet setting from location to location.

"He isn't well. He hasn't been for many years. I've paid for the best care possible, but there isn't a thing they can do to bring back his mind. He doesn't know me, doesn't recognize me." Tears rolled perfectly down her face and dripped onto the front of her tank top. "Before I left the island we had a huge fight. Things were said that couldn't be taken back, and by the next time I saw him he didn't remember me. It was too late." She swiped at her eyes, rubbing hard with the heels of her hands.

So, Constance had lost her father, too, in a sense. The baseball in my throat began to shrink. She was obviously in a lot of pain and I knew firsthand how that felt. "But, where is he? When do you see him without me knowing about it? Without *Entertainment Tonight* cameras on your tail? How did you pull this off?" I had a dozen questions but these were the ones that rolled off my tongue first. Our lives are an open book, even with the security the studio provides.

Constance smiled thinly. "You know how good I am with makeup and disguise, Grace. If I don't want to be recognized, I'm not recognized. My last name is different from my father's. You know I had it changed years ago. Magurski wasn't going to fly with the studios back then. As to where he is right now, he's in Boston in a facility for Alzheimer's patients. We can think about taking you there for a visit if you want to see him."

"Of course I want to see him. He's my grandfather." I took a deep breath and tried to understand what I had just learned about my family. My anger crouched in the background like a cat ready to pounce, but for the moment, it was overwhelmed by the need to know more. While Constance had been talking I had done some mental math and realized that if she had left the island at eighteen and had me at barely nineteen, then maybe my father had lived here as well. Just as I was about to ask, the phone on the bench that served as a coffee table rang. Constance answered it, listened a minute, put her hand over the mouthpiece, and said, "Grace, I have to take this. Why don't you go unpack?"

6. back to the future

i heaved myself out of the wicker rocker and headed to the stairs. As I passed through the foyer I heard Toffee and Camilla in the kitchen. Toffee was bemoaning the state of the "larder" as he put it. It seemed the kitchen was not stocked to his liking.

I headed upstairs, my head spinning with unanswered questions. But Constance seemed to be opening up. Maybe it was that she had come home. Maybe it was that she thought I was finally old enough to know whatever truths were out there. Whatever the reason, I felt good about it.

My backpack and duffel sat on the floor of my room. I dug around in my backpack until I unearthed my iPod, and put on an Aerosmith album. I put Froggy on the flow-ered bedspread, and the music rocked in my ears as I took another look around my mother's old room. This might be a good time to admit to going through a serious Nancy Drew phase when I was younger. I think I read all the books, much to Toffee's dismay. "They aren't classics, Grace," he used to tell me. But on the subject of Nancy Drew, he was outnumbered.

"When I was your age, the Nancy Drew books at my local library were in the first bookcase to the right of the front door and I read every single one of them," Constance had told me. I wondered now if it had been at the library here on Martha's Vineyard when she stayed with her grandparents that she escaped with Nancy. There were things I wanted to know, and what better place to begin than my mother's childhood room?

I started with the dressing table. The single drawer opened easily to reveal nothing more exciting than an emery board, a cotton-candy-pink lipstick, and a packet of Kleenex. I imagined my mother getting ready for a date and applying that lipstick, then blotting it on the tissue to leave a perfect lip print. Steven Tyler wailed in my head as I shoved the drawer closed and moved on to the bureau between the windows. As I opened the first of five drawers, my gaze was drawn to the view. A park with a gazebo stood between the house and the beach, but from my second-floor vantage point the water seemed endless. How many times had my mother stopped what she was doing to admire the waves breaking on the shore or the seagulls circling above? I made a mental note to sketch it when I had time.

The drawer was empty, as were the four that followed it. The dressing table and dresser had yielded nothing. What would Nancy Drew do next? The closet. Why not take a look? I grasped the glass knob and swung the door open.

The scent of mothballs and cedar knocked me back. The small space was empty except for a clothes bag, the canvas kind that zips closed. I took off my headset and put down my iPod. This required all my attention. I reached for the zipper and pulled. It resisted and I pulled harder. Harder still. Nothing. I leaned closer and saw that the zipper held a piece of shiny pink material in its teeth. I worked it free, and as I lowered the zipper, the bag poofed and a hot pink formal gown escaped its prison. I'm no clotheshorse but this was interesting. I fumbled around until I found the pink satin hanger and pulled the garment free of the bag and into the room. In the sunlight I saw that it was probably a prom dress. I had no real experience with formals except in movies or on television, but I had to admit it was beautiful. This was Constance's history. Her bedroom, her dried-up cotton-candy lipstick, her frothy prom dress. Had my father been her date? Had he kissed those cotton-candy lips and swirled her around a gym decorated with cheesy Kleenex flowers and crepe paper? Maybe even a disco ball?

I held the dress up to my bony frame and looked at myself in the dressing table mirror. Maybe with a little lipstick, a well-stuffed Wonder Bra, and a complete makeover, I could pull it off. I closed my eyes and swayed back and forth wondering if I would ever have a prom night, a date, a gown, and a wrist corsage. Who was I kidding?

A knock at the bedroom door brought me back to reality. "Just a minute." I laid the dress on the bed and went to the door, opening it just far enough so I could see out but nobody could see in. I wanted to keep my find a secret for the time being. It was Toffee.

"Grace, your mother wants us to go to the market, and I can't say it's any too soon. Whoever stocked—and I use the word loosely—the kitchen must live on junk food and baked beans. There's not a green vegetable to be found."

"But Toffee, I was just about to unpack."

"This is the perfect opportunity to get your bearings a bit and catch the flavor of Oak Bluffs. That's the town we're in. Let's go."

I had to admit that a chance to get to know the neighborhood could prove important. "Pay attention. You never know when you might learn something you can use," Camilla always said.

7. louise

toffee and I had a system for shopping that we had worked out long ago. He made out the list precisely on a sheet of paper, and when we got to the store he carefully folded the list in half and tore. We each took half and went on our way up and down the aisles. When I was younger I used to relish the feeling of freedom I had in the grocery store. Of course, I knew Toffee was always looking out for me, and most of the time Camilla accompanied us, but the choice between the Granny Smith apples and the Golden Delicious was mine and mine alone. If I wanted Froot Loops instead of granola, Toffee looked the other way.

It might not sound like a big thing, but grocery shopping was something normal people did. Constance would probably have had her groceries delivered like most everyone else in Tinsel Town, except that Toffee is extremely fussy about food, and Camilla is a vegan, so it was simply easier in the long run to let us do the shopping. Besides, my first lesson in fractions was learning that two halves of a grocery list made a whole list. And a whole list was guaranteed to turn into some awesome meals.

I love to cook, and I guess I came by that naturally enough. When we are at home in Beverly Hills, or if the studio puts us up in a house or condo on location, Toffee does the cooking. He's a gourmet cook and, like everything else, he uses cooking as an opportunity to teach me something. Besides fractions, I learned to follow directions by reading and following recipes, and I learned to spell by helping Toffee with shopping lists.

The town of Oak Bluffs was crowded, and the streets were clogged with vehicles, many of which carried bicycles on racks or beach equipment on top. Mopeds and bikes scooted along the side of the roads, and the scent of sea air mixed with fish added to the summery feel. Car horns, seagull cries, and the honky-tonk music I'd heard earlier all combined to make for a party atmosphere.

"There's supposed to be a wonderful market here. You know, Constance loves your peach tart, but I'm not sure exactly what all the ingredients are, so I'll let you pick those up along with your half of the list. Deal?"

"That's not fair, Toffee. That gives me more stuff to grab, and you get the advantage." Did I mention that we usually raced each other to see who could finish their half of the list first? First one to the checkout line won, and the loser had to carry the bags from the car to the house.

"Not up to the challenge, Grace?" Toffee grinned wickedly and pulled into the supermarket parking lot. I was out of the Jeep with my hands wrapped around the handle of a shopping cart before the *ding, ding* that marked Toffee locking the vehicle. There was no running in the store, but I had perfected the art of fast-walking. I paused in the entrance to get the store layout before making a sharp left to the produce section. Oranges, tomatoes, and a cantaloupe joined grapes, mangoes, and peaches in the bottom of the cart. I was reaching for a head of lettuce on the fly and looking for the peppers when I crashed head-on into another cart.

"Ugh, I'm sorry." It's difficult to speak with a cart handle jammed into your stomach.

"You should really watch where you're going." A girl about my own age righted a box of cereal and saved a loaf of bread from being permanently squashed by a bottle of laundry detergent. She raised her head to speak again, and her green eyes glittered.

"I'm sure she didn't mean to hit us." The second voice came from the floor where a woman was gathering up peaches. I squatted down to help her collect the fuzzy fruit and hide my flaming face from the girl. The woman smiled at me. "I think we got them all," she said.

We stood up and the girl took the peaches I had gathered from my hand, inspecting each one before she placed it in the cart. The woman held out her hand to me.

"I'm Sybil Herman, and this is my daughter, Louise."

"Hi, I'm Grace." I held back my last name. I had found out the hard way not to let people know who my mother was right away. My London pen pal, Liz, had fooled us all. Toffee tutored her in Latin, Camilla read her palm and predicted all kinds of good things in store for her, I felt like I had made a true friend, and Constance took her to the set one day so she could see how a movie was made. We trusted her implicitly until she took pictures of Constance sunbathing by the pool of the estate where we stayed and sold them to the newspapers. I guess Camilla was right. Good things did happen, because Liz sure made a lot of money on those pictures.

"Hi." Louise's wavy red hair hung to her shoulders, and she had multiple earrings in each ear. Her jeans rode low on her hips, and the halter she wore exposed just enough skin. She looked like she had just stepped out of a J. Crew catalog, and I was feeling very ordinary by comparison when Toffee appeared.

"Hello, I'm Reginald Toffee. Is there a problem?"

"Nothing that a traffic cop in the produce section

couldn't cure. No, really, we're fine." Mrs. Herman smiled and introduced herself and Louise.

"Grace sometimes gets carried away when we're racing. Please allow me to replace anything that was ruined. You have quite a full cart. Stocking up for the weekend?"

"No. I own a catering business and I have two parties this weekend."

My ears perked up. Catering? Parties? Food?

"What's your business called?" I was intrigued.

"Party Thyme. That's T-H-Y-M-E. I grow my own herbs. This weekend will be a little rough, though. My assistant is down with the flu, so that leaves just me and Louise."

Louise rolled her eyes and her chest heaved in a sigh that made me think she would rather be doing anything but helping her mother cater.

"I could help." The words slipped out before I knew it.

"Oh, that's very kind of you, Grace, but . . ."

"Grace is actually quite a good cook," Toffee said. "She makes a mean peach tart, and her cassoulet is to die for."

"I have to say you are probably the only teenager I know who makes cassoulet." Mrs. Herman smiled.

"Mother, we have to go. I have to babysit the triplets, remember?" Louise rocked the cart back and forth, threatening to unseat the peaches piled on top.

"Grace, I'd be happy to have you help." Mrs. Herman dug around in her purse. "Here's my business card. We live just two blocks from here. If you have trouble finding it, just ask anyone. We've lived here forever. I like to get an early start, so if you could come by around eight o'clock tomorrow morning that would be great."

"Yeah, great," said Louise, and I let myself hope that I might have found a friend. Time would tell.

8. flying horses

on the way home we passed the carousel I had been hearing, and, of course, Toffee knew all about it.

"That's the Flying Horses carousel. It's the oldest operating platform carousel in the country. There are twenty-two wooden horses with real horsehair tails and each horse has a name."

"Flying Horses?" I had heard that name somewhere before, but I couldn't put my finger on it. I turned in my seat to look back at the carousel. I planned to take a ride on one of those twenty-two wooden horses.

Since I had lost the supermarket sprint, I unloaded the food and put it away in the kitchen. Camilla pushed open the kitchen door as I folded the last paper bag and bent to put it away under the sink.

"Your mother is taking a nap. Toffee has decided on

fish and a salad for dinner. I'll make the salad unless you want to." As a vegan, Camilla was very creative with vegetables and her salads were always filled with surprising ingredients.

"I'll leave the salad to you. I'm going to unpack." With Camilla and Toffee busy in the kitchen, and my mother napping, I had time to continue my investigation. I tiptoed upstairs to my room and closed the door behind me. Froggy surveyed me from the bed. Even I had to admit that he looked a little shabby. His once emerald plush body had faded to a brownish green over the years, and he had lost one buggy eye, but I kept him with me like some people hang on to a rabbit's foot for good luck. I remembered how, when I was little, Constance used to tuck us into bed together. "Say good night, Froggy. Say good night, Gracie." I still liked it when she called me Gracie.

I had covered the dressing table, bureau, and closet. As I decided where to search next, I pulled clothes out of my duffel and stuffed them into drawers. Some things needed to be hung up. The closet yielded hangers, and as I put the garments away, my eyes strayed to the closet shelf. From my vantage point it looked empty, but there could be something shoved to the back. I stood on my toes and felt around as far as I could stretch, but that wasn't enough. I pulled over the dressing table stool and stepped up on it. Now I could see the entire shelf. Empty.

"Grace, come set the table. Dinner will be ready soon." Toffee's voice drifted up the stairs. I stepped down from the stool and returned it to its spot under the dressing table. The pillows I had scattered earlier were still on the floor and I hurriedly gathered them up. I took a step toward the bed and felt something wobble under my feet. I threw the armful of pillows onto the bed and knelt down and pushed aside the rag rug. I felt around until I found a loose board in the worn wood floor.

I worked my fingers under the edges of the board and pulled. It slid out, exposing a dark, musty-smelling rectangular hole. A perfect hiding place for things you didn't want anyone to find. What had Constance stashed here? I lay on my stomach and reached into the hole. Visions of rats and spiders danced through my head as I felt around the dusty space. Nothing. I inched forward and reached farther in all directions. Constance was taller than I am and had longer arms. If she really wanted to hide something, she could have put it well out of sight under the floor. I hitched forward and stuck my arm in so far I thought it might get stuck.

"Grace! Hurry up!" My search would have to wait.

I opened the kitchen door. Constance sat at the table, looking like she had just stepped off the set. Her hair was freshly washed and brushed and her makeup was perfect. Toffee puttered around, placing the whole fish on a large platter while Camilla tossed her salad. I grabbed place mats, dishes, and silverware and set the table. We sat down and dug in.

"Did you have a good nap, Constance?" I said. I was hoping we could continue our conversation after dinner, so it was in my best interest to be pleasant.

"I had a terrible headache, but I'm feeling better now. I hear you and Toffee had an interesting visit to the market. You've landed yourself a job?" She raised her right eyebrow and waited.

It was a well-known fact in our little family-like unit that Toffee is an incurable gossip. The time he was tricked into talking to one of the tabloids about Constance's love of Ben and Jerry's New York Super Fudge Chunk ice cream almost cost him his job. Well, to be fair, it wasn't really the story that ticked Constance off—it was the doctored picture on the front page: Constance's head on an unknown female body clad in a muumuu under the headline *CONSTANCE MEREDITH IN HIDING AFTER TIPPING SCALES AT 300 POUNDS.*

I scowled at him for telling my news and then turned to Constance. "It's the perfect summer job for me, Constance. Please don't tell me I can't do it. This isn't L.A.; nothing is going to happen to me on this little island." Constance's lips drew into a thin line, but she didn't say anything. I took this as a good sign and plunged ahead.

"Toffee met Mrs. Herman. She's really nice and her daughter is around my age. It would be really cool to have a friend here. Someone to hang out with." Constance cut a small piece of fish and speared it with her fork.

"Grace, I have my reservations about letting you work for someone I don't know, but I think it's time I let you spread your wings a little. I got my first job when I was right around your age. Besides, it is a perfect summer job for you." She popped the fish into her mouth and smiled. "I would like to meet Mrs. Herman at some point, though."

"Sure, fine. Thanks, Constance." A grin stretched my face. "Ribbit," I said.

"Ribbit," she responded. Our good mood was short lived, though.

"Well, you won't be meeting her this week," said Camilla. "I had a vision of you traveling starting tomorrow morning."

"No way. I'm on hiatus, and I'm spending time with Grace, getting to know the island again, and getting some rest. In fact, I heard from an old friend earlier today and I'm meeting her for coffee tomorrow. You're stuck with me for the next month. Now pass that salad."

I remembered the phone call that had interrupted our conversation earlier that day and was about to ask Constance about her friend when the wall phone rang. Loud. I looked at Constance, who looked at Camilla. Toffee answered the phone on the second ring and handed it to Constance.

"What are you saying, Stanley? No, absolutely not. I can't possibly leave right now. I refuse to go to New York to do a photo shoot for a movie that hasn't even wrapped."

Stanley is my mother's agent, and what he says goes. She credits him with getting her to where she is in her career, and if Stanley said she was going to New York, then all of us sitting around that table knew she was going to New York.

9. puzzle pieces

after dinner Toffee and I did the dishes so that Camilla could help Constance pack. The studio was sending a plane for her early the next morning. She had told Stanley that she didn't want to be gone for more than a day, so I was trying to look on the bright side, thinking that we would continue our talk the next evening. Besides, this turn of events gave me time to investigate the hidey-hole under the floor without interruption.

Toffee washed and I dried, and the dishes were done in no time. Toffee excused himself to read, and I took the stairs two at a time. I closed the door behind me. The pink dress was where I had left it on the bed, and the rug was rucked up against the dressing table.

I dropped to my knees, moved the board aside, and reached into the hole under the floor. I stretched and reached. I turned my head to the side on the floor. My fingertips brushed something cool, metallic, and rectangular. A box of some sort. I tried to grab it, but it was just a hair too far from my grasp. I sat up and looked around the room. A wire hanger on the floor next to my duffel caught my eye. I unwound it and formed a hook on one end. I lay on my stomach on the floor and poked the hanger toward the box. At first it just slid off but finally, when I pulled, I felt the weight of the box. I inched it close enough to grab with my fingers and pulled it toward me. It scraped along the rough wood subfloor, and the thick layer of dust covering it felt both soft and gritty under my fingers. I got it to the opening, turned it on its side, and pulled it out. The gray metal box had been hidden under the floor for a long time. I blew at the dust, which rose in clouds like smog over Los Angeles and straight up my nose. I sneezed three times. My hair fell over my face, and I brushed it back with dusty fingers.

Finally, I was able to examine my find. It was about a foot long, eight or nine inches wide, and maybe four inches deep. It had a lock, and the lock required a key. Furiously I searched the hole again, feeling all around. Maybe I would luck out and feel it hanging on a nail, or taped to the boards. No such luck. That would have been too easy. I picked up the box and shook it. Something clunked around inside but there was another sound, too, a fluttering like papers or maybe photographs.

Where would Constance have hidden the key? With

the box gripped in my hands, I looked around the room. All the drawers were empty. No help there. My eyes skimmed over my backpack and duffel bag and then moved back to them. I put down the box, walked to the duffel, and pawed through it until I found the small pouch that held my toiletries. I unzipped it and reached for the manicure kit. Inside was a nail file. Nancy Drew would have picked the lock, and I hoped to do the same.

I sat cross-legged on the floor with the box in front of me and the file in my right hand. I inserted the sharp point into the lock. I wriggled it. I poked it. I tried to turn it. The lock held and the contents of the box swished and thumped inside.

I pictured every detective movie I had ever seen. When they picked locks on the bad guy's hideouts it always looked so easy. Well, they had lots of practice. I just had to keep trying. I inserted the point again and gingerly moved it up and down and back and forth. Up, down, right, left. I tried again, moving it around this time. As I prepared to jiggle the file, my bedroom door swung open.

Constance padded in on bare feet across the floor. I had been so engrossed I hadn't heard her knock. I shoved the box under the bed and hoped she hadn't heard the slight scraping of metal against wood.

"Grace, I'll be leaving early in the morning. I wanted to say good-bye. I hope you enjoy your first trip into the working world." She smiled and took a step toward the bed. "I see you found my prom dress. I had forgotten that was still in the closet." She reached out and smoothed the skirt. "What a night that was." It was almost as if she was talking to herself.

The familiar ache began in the vicinity of my heart. What could it hurt to ask? "Constance, who did you go to the prom with?"

Her back was still to me and she stiffened as if weighing my question. After what seemed like hours, she turned around and went back to her seat at the dressing table. When her eyes met mine I saw the pain there and almost took the question back, but the hurt around my heart wouldn't let me. We stared at each other until, finally, Constance dropped her eyes.

"I went to the prom with your father, Grace. He was very handsome in his tuxedo. It was one of the last times we were really happy together." She peered at me, her eyes squinched up. "Grace, what's that all over your face?"

"My face?" I was suddenly aware that my hands were filthy from handling the box. There must be dirt on my face from when I pushed back my hair. She ran her hand through her thick hair and opened her mouth as if to say more when the phone rang again. Constance and I both jumped a little. She grabbed the phone by the bed.

"Hello? Yes, Stanley. I know, Stanley. Stanley, hang
." Constance put her hand over the receiver. "Grace,
sorry. I have to take this. When you hear me get on the

other line, hang this one up, will you?" She left my room as silently as she had arrived. I sat numbly with the phone in my hand. I had an answer, only one about my father, but an answer nevertheless. He had lived here, too. They had been high school sweethearts.

"Grace, hang up the extension." Constance's voice came through the phone line. I replaced the receiver on the cradle, stood up, and walked down the hall to her room. I had questions that needed answers. Now. Without knocking, I pushed open her bedroom door just as she was hanging up the phone.

"I have a right to know who my father is. I've waited long enough." My heart pounded in my ears. Constance looked at me for a long moment.

"Yes, Grace. You do have a right to know who your father is, but there is more to the story than just a name and tonight is not the time to go into it."

"But . . ."

"Grace, I said not tonight. When we have this discussion I want to do it right, and I don't have time tonight."

I spit out one syllable, "Fine," turned on my heel, and left the room, slamming the door behind me. Tears threatened but I blinked them away. When I got back to my room and closed the door, I sat down on the floor and reached under the bed for the box. I would get my own answers. Constance always said we didn't need father—well, right then I felt like I didn't need her. I placed my hands on either side of the box's lid and pulled up. Still locked. I put the box down and looked for the file. Where had it gone? I searched on top of the bed, among the many pillows. Froggy eyed me.

"You're a big help." My bare foot skidded over something sharp and thin. I swooped the file up, settled once more on the floor, and put the box in my lap. Up, down, rattle. In, out, jiggle. Around, and around. Right, left, click. Once more I put my hands on either side of the box's top and lifted. It gave.

I felt like I was spying on my mother naked. This wasn't my property. I should close it now and put it back under the floor where Constance had placed it so many years earlier. A small voice in the back of my head said that, in a way, this was my property if it contained anything that would help me find my father. The father that Constance had refused to talk about until tonight and then not given me the answers I wanted. Why shouldn't I know as much as I could about him? Why should I have to wait for her to feel the time was right? To feel that I was old enough? Or that there was time to tell the story, whatever it was, properly? After all, he was *my* father and I was fifteen. In some cultures I would have been married with children already. I took a deep breath and opened the box.

"Well, Grace. I see you found my hiding place."

10. party thyme

i slammed the top back down. There was no use trying to hide what I was doing this time. The rug was pushed into a multicolored lump next to the dressing table, the loose board lay half under the bed, and the metal box nested in my lap. I hung my head and slumped. Maybe if I made myself small enough she wouldn't notice me.

"You know I pay good money to have this house kept spotless. I couldn't figure out how your hands and face would have gotten so dirty in this room and then I remembered my hidey-hole. I hid that box on prom night." Constance crossed the room and stood in front of me. I found myself staring at the deep rose polish on her toenails until she squatted down in front of me. "Have you opened it?"

My throat clamped down and I choked out the words.

"No. I found it and picked the lock but I didn't look inside yet. Honest." I lifted my head and looked her square in the eyes. "I want to, though. I deserve to know about my father. You owe me that, Mother." I clamped down hard on the box and pulled it to me. Tears burned behind my eyes. I blinked them away.

"You will know everything in good time but not tonight." She sighed and reached out her hands. "Give me the box, Grace. The things inside belong to me." Her voice was soft with an iron lining. A voice I knew well. I gave her the box. She stood up. "I'll call you from New York. I want to hear all about your first day of work." She put one arm around my shoulders. I sat stiffly, not giving in to her hug. "Gracie, I know this is difficult. I know you have questions that I haven't answered, but when the time comes I want to do it right." I was silent. Her lips brushed my hair and then she was gone. Gone with the box that held some answers. If only I hadn't stormed into her room demanding she talk to me and stayed here, I would have had the box unlocked and opened earlier.

I looked at my grimy hands for a long time before I decided that a shower could wait until morning. It had been a very long day. I pulled off my jeans, padded to the bathroom on bare feet, and brushed my teeth and washed my hands and face. I climbed into bed under sheets, bedspread, and prom dress—and with the rest of my clothes still on—thinking I would lie awake all night mulling over the things I had learned that day.

the next thing I knew the sun was streaming through the window into my eyes and it was 7:30. I had half an hour to get to Louise's house. It wouldn't be a good move to be late on my first day. I flung back the covers, scattering fancy pillows and Froggy to the floor, and rushed to the bathroom. As the shower beat down on my head I let my mind wander for just a moment to the events of the day before. Constance had left for New York, but the box was probably here, somewhere in her room. Would I have an opportunity to find it, go through it, and replace it before she came back? How else could I find out about my father? I toweled off and crossed the hall to my room. Despite the number of times I had told Toffee and Camilla I was going to unpack I hadn't finished. Some of my clothes were still jammed in my duffel in a wrinkled wad, but there was nothing to do about it now. I pulled out a pair of shorts, a shirt that looked reasonably clean, and a pair of platform flip-flops, which I quickly replaced with sneakers. A more comfortable choice.

I pounded down the stairs and into the kitchen. Camilla sat at the table drinking the soy concoction she started each day with, while Toffee ground beans for fresh coffee.

"Toffee, can you drive me to Louise's house? I'm going to be late. I have the address, and Mrs. Herman said they lived near the market."

"You need to eat something, Grace. Breakfast is the most important meal of the day," Toffee said.

"I don't have time. Besides, I'll be working with food all day, remember? I'm sure there will something I can eat."

Toffee looked longingly at the coffeepot. "OK, let's go."

We drove through the campground, past the carousel, silent at this time of morning, past the market, and soon pulled up in front of a charming, weathered gray house surrounded by a white picket fence that formed an arbor in front. Pink roses climbed the arbor toward the sun.

"Thanks, Toffee. I think I can find my way home. See you later." I closed the Jeep door and walked under the arbor and up the brick walk followed by the sweet scent of roses. The red front door opened before I could knock.

"Hey. Come on in. Mom is getting things set up in the kitchen." Louise's red curls were pulled back from her face, making her cat's eyes even more prominent. She wore jeans and a T-shirt. She yawned and stretched as I followed her down a hall from the front of the house to the back. "I can't believe you really want to do this. It's so boring."

"I like to cook. I think I might want to be a chef when I get older."

Louise made a noise between a snort and a hiss as she pushed open the swinging door to the kitchen. The smell of cinnamon made my mouth water.

"Something smells good," I said. Mrs. Herman stood behind the island in the middle of the room.

"Good morning, Grace. I made cinnamon buns. I figured if you're anything like Louise, you probably left the house without breakfast."

As we gobbled breakfast buns and drank freshly squeezed orange juice, Mrs. Herman bustled around the kitchen setting up workstations.

"OK, we're going to do the prep for Saturday's afternoon party first. This is a long-time island resident, and she wants a simple but elegant picnic for thirty people."

"Is it Lacy Thomas?" Louise interrupted. I recognized the name of a famous pop singer.

"Well, yes, actually it is, but let's not name-drop, shall we? I treat all my clients the same. I'm hoping you will be able to help us set up and serve tomorrow, Grace. We sure could use a hand. Lacy's party is in the afternoon, and then in the evening I have new clients and I'd like to make a good impression. This business depends a lot on word of mouth."

"Sure, I'd be happy to help out."

"Well, all right then. Let's get busy. Grace, I've set you up over there. We need to peel some potatoes, and Louise,

I'm depending on you to make the veggie tray look other-worldly. I'll get busy with the pecan tarts."

For a while the only sounds were the potato peeler scraping off potato skins, the chopping and cutting sounds coming from Louise's station, and the thump and roll as Mrs. Herman rolled out pie crust.

"You really want to be a chef?" Louise was cutting radishes into roses.

"It's something I've thought about doing. Why? What do you want to be?"

"A journalist. I have a part-time summer job with the *Vineyard Gazette* working on the 'Who's in Town?' column."

My radar went up, and I tried to keep my voice in the normal range when I asked, "What's that?"

"It's the column that comes out once a week telling what celebrities have been spotted that week. We get a lot of stars here in the summer, you know." Louise smiled and kept cutting.

I wanted to sink into the floor and disappear. The only kid my age I met on this island, and she was a reporter in training for *The National Enquirer.* Suddenly I was glad that Constance was in New York.

"So, don't you want to know who's been spotted this week?"

"Uh, sure."

"Constance Meredith. You know, the movie star? She

is so cool. I can't wait for her latest movie to come out. The one about vampires. I'd love to interview her."

Swell, not just a journalist but a fan, too. I really knew how to pick them.

"You know, I went to high school with her. Of course her name was Magurski, but she was beautiful even back then. Louise, she's really coming home and people shouldn't bother her." Mrs. Herman opened the oven door and put in a tray of pecan tarts that looked mouth-watering. Then it clicked. She had gone to school with Constance. That meant she knew my father, too.

"Wow, that's cool that you knew her way back then," I said. "What was she like?"

"Well, we didn't exactly run in the same circles. She was only here a couple of years as I recall, but she was very popular. She certainly caught the boys' attention."

"Ouch, damn it! I hate cutting vegetables!" Louise threw down her knife and grabbed her left hand.

"Let me see." Mrs. Herman never flinched. She took Louise's hand in hers, ran cold water over it, and inspected the cut. "It's not bad. Wrap this around it and I'll get a Band-Aid." She gave Louise a clean kitchen towel and disappeared through the kitchen door.

"I really hate helping. No offense. I can tell you even like peeling potatoes but I'd rather be anywhere but here," Louise said.

Before I could respond, Mrs. Herman returned, Band-Aid in hand. "Maybe you two should take a break. Louise, why don't you show Grace around town?"

"Sure. What do you want to see?" she asked.

"The carousel. I'd really like to see the carousel." Louise looked at me like I was the biggest dork on the face of the earth.

"That is so for babies. But OK. Sometimes the stars bring their kids there and I get a sighting." When her hand was bandaged, we promised Mrs. Herman we'd be back in an hour and left the house through the back door. We'd walked less than a block before the calliope music of the carousel drifted out over the town.

"You know, my mother was jealous of Constance Meredith in high school." Louise's red hair blew away from her face like a brightly colored windsock. Her earrings sparkled and her eyes hid behind dark sunglasses. We stepped off the curb across from the carousel and I opened my mouth to ask what she meant, when the blaring of a horn made us both jump and scream. Bearing down on us and showing no sign of slowing was an SUV the size of the *Queen Mary*. Louise grabbed my arm and dragged me with her back to the safety of the sidewalk. The vehicle continued on, pelting us with road gravel in its wake before it stopped and the driver's window whirred down.

"Watch where you're walking. You want to get killed?"

The driver leaned out his window and scowled back at us before he peeled out.

"Are you OK, Grace? That idiot Mike Sutton. Shouldn't even have a driver's license the way he flies around here." Louise flipped him the bird, and this time we looked both ways before crossing the street to the Flying Horses.

11. the brass ring

every wooden horse on the carousel had a rider. The tinkling music washed over me, and I couldn't help but smile. Now this was normal. A carousel ride in the summer. Cotton candy vendors twirled pink clouds of spun sugar on paper cones and poured brightly colored syrup over crushed ice to make slushes. Camilla, health-food fiend extraordinaire, would have covered her eyes to avoid even the sight of such junk, but I felt great just being another tourist.

"Let's get a slush and some cotton candy." I reached into my pocket for money before I remembered that I didn't have any. I never carried cash, because Constance was always signing for things or Toffee or Camilla were with me and had the platinum card or we were on an expense account through the studio. Louise saw me fumbling in my pocket and coming up empty.

"My treat." She turned to the loosely formed line in front of the cotton candy vendor. I followed, feeling like a clueless excuse for a teenage girl.

"Look, I'll pay you back." I hoped that Louise wouldn't think I was too lame to hang out with.

"No problem. Let's get this stuff and get out of here. You've seen the carousel now and it's so not cool to be seen here if you're over nine years old." She flipped her hair and looked over the top of her sunglasses at the little kids racing to get in line for a ride.

"Can we take just one ride? Really, I'll pay you back."

"You're kidding. Well, sure. I guess. But what's the big deal?" Louise shoved a cloud of cotton candy into my hand and held up an enormous slush with two straws. "These are big. We can share," she said.

"It's just that I've never been on a carousel before." As my face flamed with embarrassment, Louise hooked her index finger over her sunglasses and pulled them farther down on her nose. Her green eyes moved up and down me like I was some sort of vermin and she was the exterminator.

"Are you, like, afraid of rides or something?" Louise pulled a hunk of cotton candy off the paper cone and rolled it between her fingers. She popped it into her mouth and washed it down with a slurp of purple slush.

"No. I just never had the chance before. Not everyone lives in a town with a carousel in the middle of it, you know."

"OK, you don't need to get all defensive about it." Louise pushed her sunglasses back up and I couldn't see her eyes, but I suspected they were rolling. She slurped through the straw and offered me what was left. I took it and pulled hard on the straw.

"Owwww." I held my hand to my forehead.

Louise smirked. "Brain freeze? I hate those."

She finished the slush and I devoured the rest of the cotton candy.

"Come on, I'll get the tickets. Let's get this kid stuff over with."

When our turn came to ride, Louise chose a large white horse with violet eyes. "I always ride Henry L," she said.

I clambered onto the brown horse next to hers. "Henry L, what's so special about him?"

"The band Flying Horses took their name and their stage names from this carousel. Henry L is the lead singer. Haven't you ever heard of them? Their picture is hanging over by the pinball machine."

Louise's explanation jogged my memory. "They paint their faces, right? I'm not a fan."

"Well, they've been around forever. You must be into the boy bands."

"No, I like classic rock, but only certain bands like the Stones and Aerosmith and some Beatles."

"When we get back to the house I'll show you my album collection."

Albums? I thought longingly about my albums and turntable at our house in Beverly Hills. Maybe we were kindred spirits after all. Louise was still talking. "Grab the brass ring and you get a free ride. There are a bunch of rings hanging on the rod over there. You'll see them when you come around. Some people believe if you get the brass ring, you get a wish, too, but that's never worked for me." The ride lurched into motion and the music grew louder and louder as the carousel moved faster and faster. I leaned for the rings the first time around and missed. The second time I held on tight with my left hand, stretched, and pulled the brass ring free with my right. Louise gave me a grin and a thumbs-up. I closed my hand around the ring and wished for answers to all my questions.

12. out of our heads

"you can get a free ride if you turn that ring in. I'll wait for you." Louise slouched next to one of the arcade games, swinging her sunglasses in her hand and looking too cool for words.

"I think I'll hang on to it for good luck. We should probably be getting back. Didn't we tell your mother we'd only be gone an hour?"

We left the carousel building and walked toward Louise's house. On the corner where we had almost been creamed by the SUV stood a tall blond girl and two teenage boys.

"Oh, great," muttered Louise. She pushed against my shoulder as if to steer me in another direction, but we had already been seen.

"Hey, Herman, been riding the carousel? Isn't that too sweet for words. Who's your little friend?" The girl grinned at each boy in turn, shot out her right hip, and twirled a lock of her long blond hair around her finger.

"What's wrong, Tanya? Only two Stooges today? Is Moe sick?" We kept walking.

"How's your boyfriend? Oh, that's right, he dumped you for me." She put her hand to her mouth and opened her eyes wide in mock sympathy.

"Your thong must be on too tight, Tanya. I kicked Billy to the curb long before you got your talons into him. Let's go, Grace."

Tanya's laughter followed us, echoed by the boys' deeper chuckles.

When we had put a block between them and us, I figured it was safe to speak. "Who was that?"

"*That* was Tanya Sutton. Daughter of the moron who almost ran us over. Isn't she a sweetheart? Sort of a cross between Barbie and a hyena. She's God's gift to this island. Just ask her. She'll tell you."

I thought twice about asking more and decided to wait.

We arrived at Louise's, pushed open the front door, and followed the hall to the kitchen where the delicious aroma of pecan tart filled the air. Mrs. Herman was just taking a large tray of the tarts out of the oven. She deposited it on the counter and wiped a strand of hair from her forehead.

"Just in time, girls." She put us to work and once again the sounds of chopping, mixing, scraping, and rolling filled the house. I diced potatoes and onions and mixed a huge potato salad for Lacy Thomas's picnic.

"That's right, Grace. Nice job. How did you get so interested in cooking? Your father seemed to know his way around the supermarket. Is he a chef?"

Well, who knew? Maybe he was. "Um, yeah, you might say that," I replied, before hastily changing the subject. "You know, it's way cool that you went to high school with Constance Meredith." I tossed the potato mixture together and held my breath.

"Well, like I said, we didn't really hang out with the same crowd. I grew up here, so I knew just about everyone. Constance was the new kid for a while, and even in a small school that's tough. Why, I remember when she tried out for cheerleader and didn't make the squad. Hard to believe, huh?"

Not so hard to believe if you knew what I know—how many personal trainers, stunt doubles, and exercise gurus Constance had employed over the years to help her become more graceful. At least I knew why I was such a klutz and who I got it from. "Yeah, hard to believe," I said.

By the end of the day we had filled many huge containers with food. Mrs. Herman had set out the chafing dishes, flatware, and platters to be loaded into the van the following day.

"I'm dying to see your record collection," I reminded Louise.

I followed her up the creaky, narrow stairs. She pushed open a door and stood aside. It was nothing like the room I was staying in. The walls were painted deep purple, from what I could see of them. Almost every square inch was covered with posters of old rock bands. The Stones leered at me from above a bed covered in a snarl of sheets and blankets. A tattered teddy bear peeked out from under one of the pillows. It felt good to know I wasn't the only one with a security blanket. Aerosmith kept watch over a small wooden desk that held a computer and printer. Album covers were arranged in a half moon above the dressing table mirror and Flying Horses strutted their stuff on the closet door, their painted faces looking eerily clownlike. Louise swept a pile of clothes from a beanbag chair. I plunked into it, and for the first time, noticed the bookcase under the window seat. It sagged under the weight of record albums, and a turntable sat on top connected to speakers that would look antique to most kids.

"Wow, I really love your room." I meant it, too. Louise sank down in front of the bookcase.

"What's your favorite rock album? I bet I have it here." She was nothing if not sure of herself, but I was equally sure she was wrong.

"My all-time favorite is *Out of Our Heads*."

"The Stones," Louise sniffed. "You'll have to do better than that to stump me." She flipped through the albums until she found what she was looking for. "Nineteen sixty-four and it's in mint condition. I found it at a garage sale. I don't play it, though, but lucky for you I do have the CD. Look in the pile next to your chair. It's one of my favorites, too."

We spent the next couple of hours in the world of rock and roll and would probably have stayed there longer if Louise's mother hadn't come to the door.

"Grace, it's getting dark. What time were your parents expecting you home? I'd be happy to drive you."

Whoops. She couldn't drive me, because it was a pretty sure bet that if the paparazzi that had taken our picture the day before knew where to find us, then the island natives certainly knew Constance's house.

"That's OK. I can walk and I have time to make my curfew." As I hustled down the steps, Louise called after me, "Hey, want to hang out tomorrow? Meet me in front of the carousel at eleven. I'll show you the rest of our thriving metropolis before we have to get to the first party."

I found my way past the carousel and wandered through the campground. Chinese lanterns flickered from every porch. The smell of hamburgers cooking on backyard grills made my mouth water, and the quiet sound of conversation reached my ears. I smiled as I climbed the steps to my house. I hoped I had made a friend that day.

13. the locals

i rolled out of bed and into the shower at 10:00 the next morning. I had an hour before meeting Louise. I was starving. I hoped that Toffee had made his delicious French toast. That would really hit the spot. My stomach growled and I rinsed off and wrapped a towel around myself.

I raked my fingers through my dark blond hair and wished for the millionth time that I had inherited Constance's glorious mane. My hair hung lank and stringy around my face, and no matter what goop or miracle product I tried, nothing seemed to work for more than an hour or two. I hurried across the hall looking for something semi-cool to wear. Louise had looked so catalog perfect each time I'd seen her that I thought it couldn't hurt for me to take a little more interest in my own looks. Mrs.

Herman had said we would wear uniforms of some sort to serve at the parties, but I wanted to look good to hang out with Louise.

I decided on a pair of low-rider shorts, a blue and green striped halter top, and black platform flip-flops. I started out the bedroom door when I remembered something and went back in to dig through the pockets of the shorts I'd worn the day before. I found the brass ring and slid it into my right front pocket. Good luck charms only work if you carry them with you.

Something smelled good in the direction of the kitchen, and my stomach responded. When I opened the door my eyes went straight to the plate of pancakes that sat waiting on the table. Toffee and Camilla had eaten long ago, but they were still sitting in their usual places, and Camilla was sipping her soy. Toffee had made it his business as official family chef to learn some vegan recipes for Camilla that weren't too much of a gag-fest for the rest of us. I just hoped these were not soy-based pancakes. As much as I respected Camilla's stand to help the environment and save animals, I did enjoy a good breakfast.

"Good morning, Grace. Sit down and your pancakes will be ready soon. I bought real maple syrup at the market and it is fabulous," said Toffee. "And these aren't vegan." He glanced at Camilla and smiled. She didn't smile back.

"Your mother called from New York after you went

to bed last night," Camilla said. "She will be back tonight. She thought you might like to go to the beach tomorrow. Maybe you could bring your new friend. She's safe you know. I can tell."

I didn't remind Camilla she had said the same thing about London Liz. And there was Louise's writing gig at the local newspaper to consider. I figured even a psychic can be wrong once in a while. "Yeah, that sounds great. I'll ask Louise today." I wolfed down my pancakes and scraped back my chair. "Gotta go. Louise is going to show me around and then we have those two parties. Mrs. Herman said she would bring me home." She had said no such thing but I was sure she would offer and I would have to think of a way to say no, but that was hours from now and there was no use in having Toffee and Camilla worry about me. "Oh, I could use some money. Just in case, you know?"

Toffee produced some bills from his starched khakis. "Here you go. Don't spend it all in one place." He smiled and winked.

"See you later," I called as the screen door slammed behind me. What an awesome sound.

Louise stood on the corner across from the carousel looking like something from *Cosmo Girl*. I ran my hands through my still-damp hair and stood up straighter. Her frayed cutoffs were faded just right, and the Hawaiian print bikini top showed off her tan. Her hair was tousled perfectly, like she had just rolled out of bed and onto a magazine cover, unlike mine, which simply reflected the fact that I had just rolled out of bed and nothing more. I knew how long that look took. I'd seen it done in some of the best salons in Beverly Hills. Her numerous earrings sparkled, and her fingernails and toenails were painted a brilliant shade of green.

"Hey, you look great. How did you get so tan? I thought redheads burned."

Louise laughed. "It's not a beach tan, it's Fake and Bake."

The clueless look on my face must have given me away.

"You know, from a tanning salon. Are you from Mars or something?"

"Actually, where I come from there's a tanning booth on every corner. I'd just never heard it called that before. So, what's up? What are we going to do? Speaking of your hair, I love it." My hair flopped into my face and I pushed it out. "I wish I could do something with mine. Nothing seems to work."

"I have an idea. Do you have money today?"

"Oh, yeah." I dug around in my pocket for the bills Toffee had given me. "How much do I owe you from yesterday?"

"Don't worry about that; I said it was my treat. Come on." I followed Louise up the street until she stopped in front of a small shop. THE BEAUTY BARN was stenciled on the front window. "Mary Beth is the best cutter on the island. You don't need an appointment and she'll fix you right up."

"The Beauty Barn? I don't think so." First off, it was more the size of a shed than a barn. But I suppose that "The Beauty Shed" doesn't present a very good image; although, why anyone would want to get their hair done in a barn is beyond me. Would people come out of there looking like livestock? Besides, I've been buffed, shampooed, waxed, and manicured by Hollywood's best, and even their magic generally lasted only as long as whatever star-studded event Constance was dragging me to. When I awoke the next morning, I was like Cinderella: the coach had turned back into a pumpkin and I was myself again.

"Come on. I'm telling you, she knows what she's doing. She trims my hair every six weeks." Louise tossed her head and her hair fell perfectly into place.

"OK, I guess it couldn't hurt to try."

Louise pushed open the door and a cloud of chemical fumes assaulted us.

"Hello, Louise. I don't have you down until next week. Who's your friend?" Mary Beth, a tall, thin woman with flaming orange hair, fingernails to match, and pointy glasses decorated with rhinestones, descended on us. Think Lucille Ball to the tenth power. She passed us and began tightly rolling the thin white hair of the elderly lady seated in a swivel chair who was covered from chin to ankles in a black plastic cape highlighted with gold sunbursts.

"This is Grace Toffee. We were hoping you could fit her in for a cut."

I winced at the last name Louise had assumed was mine but I didn't correct her.

"Sure thing. Just give me a few minutes to get Mrs. Hughes rolled up and under the dryer. Take a seat and look through my books until you find something you like. I can cut any style," she said to me.

We sat down on a turquoise sectional couch that had seen better days. I flipped through a book with glossy pictures of hair styles that covered everything from the ridiculous to the sublime (Toffee's phrase), until Louise said, "Stop, that's it. Everyone at school, including me, wants their hair like that." The model's hair had been cut in long layers and angled toward her chin. The back was short and tight to her head, forming a shiny helmet effect. "It's so retro. I love it."

"My hair will never do that."

"You have the perfect hair for that cut. Mine is too wavy and thick."

I watched Mary Beth seat the older woman under the dryer and set the timer. That accomplished, she approached us. "That's a perfect style for you, honey. I can do that, no problem. Go sit in my chair."

I sat in the chair recently vacated by the woman under the dryer and came to the conclusion that The Beauty Barn was a one-woman show. Mary Beth shook out a plastic cape and fastened it around me. Her scissors flashed around my head.

"Louise, did you hear that Constance Meredith is back in town? Have you spotted her for that little column you write? Oh, and Curt Shelton and Ashley Hawkins are here, too."

"Oh, I spotted Curt and Ashley at The Black Dog and they were really nice and gave me a couple of good lines for this week's column. I haven't seen Constance Meredith, but we're working two celebrity parties today, so I'm hoping maybe she'll be at one of them and I can get a real sighting and maybe a quote," said Louise.

"Well, good luck to you. I knew Constance when she was a kid here in the campground. Nice enough I suppose, until she fell in with those Up Islanders."

I was listening with every pore and about to ask what on earth an Up Islander was when Mary Beth clicked on the blow dryer. She blew and combed and brushed and sprayed for what seemed like an eternity. Pictures of starlets from the sixties with bubblelike hair flashed through my mind and I inwardly groaned. She had turned me away from the mirror and I couldn't see what she was doing. I looked to Louise for a sign, but her face was blank.

"There you go, honey. Told you I could do it." Mary Beth whirled the chair around and there I was—or at least I think it was me. The cut was perfect. Where a little while earlier flat, finger-combed hair had existed, I now sported the same perfect look the model in the style book wore. I looked like me but different, better, almost cool.

"Told you," said Louise. "Hurry up and pay. I have another idea." I pulled the bills from my pocket, paid Mary Beth, and gave her a good tip.

"Mary Beth, you said something about Constance Meredith falling in with Up Islanders. What are Up Islanders?"

"People who come from Up Island, the other end of the island from here."

"What's wrong with them? Why was it a bad thing for her to fall in with them?" I held my breath waiting for the answer.

"Why, there's nothing wrong with them as a group but with Constance it was different. She—"

Buzzzzzzzzz.

"Oh! Time to get Mrs. Hughes out from under the dryer before she evaporates. Enjoy your hair, honey." And Mary Beth was off like a red tornado.

14. piercings and body art

"**where to** now?" I couldn't help looking at my reflection in every window we passed. My hair bounced and shone. I felt great.

"Here," said Louise. I read the sign in front of the establishment: PIERCING, TATTOOS, BODY ART BY BILL.

"Bill isn't tattooing or piercing me," I said.

"First off, Bill doesn't live here anymore. His ex-wife, Marcy, does all the work now. Second, you have to be the only fifteen-year-old on the planet who doesn't have pierced ears."

I had to admit she probably had a point there, and, while I shuddered at the thought of a needle coming anywhere near me, I couldn't help noticing the sun glinting off Louise's earrings—five in the right ear, seven in the left. I took a deep breath and decided it was high time I joined the twenty-first century.

"OK, but only one hole in each ear. That's it," I said. A bell tinkled above the door as we entered. A raven-haired woman was bent over a man lying on a table that looked like the kind they use in a doctor's examining room. She had what I could only assume was a tattoo needle or a dentist's drill in her hand. A frown crossed her face when she saw us.

"Louise, I told you I can't pierce your navel until you're eighteen or until I have written permission from your mother."

"Relax, Marcy. We're here for my friend, Grace. She just wants her ears pierced. I know you can do that."

"Not until I'm finished with Steve, here." She was finishing up a series of Chinese symbols that ran from his right wrist clear up to his shoulder and around his neck. "Tilt your head, Steve, unless you want this symbol for love to end up between your eyes." She had a sense of humor, which I saw as a good sign if she was coming at me with a needle. "OK, big boy. You're all set. You know the drill. Keep it clean, don't pick at it, and if you have any questions come in and see me."

"Thanks, Marcy. You're the best." Steve heaved himself off the table and pulled on a shirt that he didn't button. The tails flapped behind him as he left.

Marcy pulled the paper cover off the table and replaced it with a fresh one. "OK, Grace, you're next." Apparently I didn't move fast enough for her. She patted the table. "Come on, this isn't going to hurt." I still hesitated. Louise shook her head and tossed her hair behind her ears and I saw those glittering earrings again.

"Let me tell you girls about the first time I ever had my ears pierced," Marcy said. "I was fifteen and my friend used two ice cubes to numb my ears before she rammed a safety pin through to make the holes. They aren't even. One is higher than the other. See?" I grimaced and my stomach turned over at the thought of putting a safety pin through my ear. Marcy moved her head back and forth just a little and I could see that the hole in her right ear was indeed higher than the one in her left.

"That's a great story, Marcy. Just be sure you make Grace's holes even."

"OK, let's get this done."

Marcy came at me with a piercing gun—only I didn't know that's what it was.

"What's that?" I pulled back, and the paper on the table crinkled under my thighs. The woman was going to shoot me.

"Relax, Grace. It's a piercing gun." Marcy smiled. "Now hold still while I mark your ears with Magic Marker to be sure I get everything lined up."

She marked my lobes and then shoved a box of stud earrings in front of me. "Choose the ones you like best.

You'll be wearing them for a while until your ears heal. See, I load the earrings up in the gun and shoot them through your ear. You won't feel a thing."

"Take the sapphires. They match your eyes," said Louise.

"You have gorgeous eyes. Very unusual. Anybody ever tell you that before?" Marcy asked.

Only about a million times, I thought.

Marcy loaded up the sapphires, and about five seconds later they were in my ears. "Use this a couple times a day and turn the earrings often to keep the holes open." She handed me a tube of antiseptic, went behind the counter, and tallied up my bill.

I handed her the money. "Here you go. Thanks, Marcy."

The bell above the door tinkled behind us. "We should probably get going. We have a lot of stuff to load and unload and set up for the picnic party. You look really nice. It was a fun morning." Louise lowered her shades on her nose in what was fast becoming a familiar gesture.

"Yeah, it was a good morning." I shook my head and gingerly touched my ears. There was just a little soreness but nothing drastic. Maybe next time I'd get the cartilage done. The little gold rings that Louise wore high up on her ears looked really neat.

"Hey, I have an idea for later tonight, after the second party. There's a club down by the ferry landing that gets some really good bands and tonight it's a bunch of old rockers. Can you get out without your parents knowing? The first set isn't until midnight."

Getting out without my "parents" knowing would be no problem. Getting out without Toffee and Camilla catching on was another thing entirely, but if I said no Louise might think I was a big chicken, and we were really starting to get along. I liked having a real friend that I had made for myself instead of some set-up Internet friend that Toffee found for me.

"OK, let's do it."

"You're on. I can get us in. I know the bouncer's brother from school. We can meet at the gazebo at midnight."

15. busted

we had arrived at Louise's, and her mother was already loading stuff into the minivan that said PARTY THYME on the driver's side door. "Let's go, girls. I've laid out your uniforms on Louise's bed. Grace, I'm sure that my assistant Carole's will fit you." For the first time, I noticed that Mrs. Herman was wearing a pair of khaki pants, boat shoes, and a green golf shirt with the Party Thyme logo embroidered on the upper left chest.

"That's kind of a cute outfit," I said to Louise.

"Yeah, that's really my style. I love looking like I'm a caddy searching for her golfer. Let's go get dressed." She rolled her eyes, turned, and headed into the house.

Lacy Thomas's picnic went off without a hitch. The food was delicious. Louise and I served some famous faces and some not-so-famous ones. Constance would have been right at home among them, and I wondered if she had been invited. While we were in the kitchen loading our trays with dessert, Louise said, "I heard some people talking about Constance Meredith. Two guys down by the beach were actually saying they heard that *Vampire's Revenge* was going to bomb and that it was coming in way over budget."

Louise balanced the heavy tray on her fingertips. "Open the door for me, will you? Man, I wish I could interview half the people here."

"Why can't you?"

"Because it's a private party and my mother insists that even stars deserve their privacy. As if. . . . Come on, this tray is getting heavy. Open the door."

When the last dish was gathered up and the last compliment on a job well done given and received, we packed up the van and drove the few miles to Louise's house to unload the remnants of the first party and load up the food for the second. As I carried a stack of chafing dishes to the van, I realized I didn't know who was hosting this party.

"So, where are we going now?"

"Well, Grace, this is a party at the summer home of a very famous actress. She comes here every summer and really guards her privacy. If I'm to stay in her good graces it's important we treat her in a professional fashion."

"So, who is it?"

Mrs. Herman acted as if she hadn't heard the question. "Let's go, girls. This is an important event and it wouldn't do to be late."

"But . . ." I began.

"Don't bother," Louise said. "I don't even know who it is. If I did, I'd tell you, but my mother was afraid I'd leak it to the paper so it's all a big mystery until we get there. I have a hunch, though."

We careened through the dusk down narrow roads bordered by stone walls and pastures until the van made a sharp right down a dirt lane. At the end was a large clapboard-covered house that seemed to ramble on forever. When I opened the door I heard waves breaking on the shore.

"This is one of the best places on the island to watch the sunset. Too bad we don't have time to enjoy it. Oh, there's our hostess now." Mrs. Herman hurried up the walkway toward the woman coming toward her. When the sun that was blinding me dipped behind a cloud, I got a clear look at our client and my knees went rubbery. It was one of my mother's closest friends. I had been to her many other homes, swum in her pools with her children. Eavesdropped on her tearful conversations with my mother when her marriage ended, and her more upbeat conversations when she found herself a "friend" half her age. I wondered briefly if he was with her. That would be a real coup for Louise. They had made the covers of everything from the tabloids to *People* to *House and Garden*. If she spotted me, my cover would be instantly blown and Louise would hate me for not trusting her.

I ducked into the back of the van and tried to look busy among the pots and pans while Louise struggled with a huge container of gazpacho.

"Give me a hand, Grace. This is heavy. Did you *see* who the hostess is? It's Lindsey Leary. Can you *believe it?*" If her voice went up one more octave, I was sure dogs from all corners of the island would come running. "I wonder if I can use this as an official celebrity spotting since I actually saw her before the party? Come on, we have to get this into the house."

I held my half of the plastic container high to hide my face. The liquid inside sloshed and made it difficult to balance.

"Come on, quit fooling around. If we drop this I'll be grounded for a month and you'll never peel another potato for Sybil Herman."

I ducked my head and kept walking. We were almost past the two women conversing about how to set up the food stations when Louise's mother called out.

"Girls, hold up for a minute. I want you to meet our client."

My throat felt like a hand had wrapped around it and squeezed. I couldn't breathe, I couldn't hear. I felt like I was underwater.

"Ms. Leary, this is my daughter, Louise, and her new friend, Grace Toffee. Grace, dear, look up and say hello."

Slowly, I raised my head, and when my eyes met Lindsey's, I tried to will her not to say anything, not to recognize me. Maybe the new hair and the earrings would act like Clark Kent's glasses did to his Superman identity.

"Why, it's Grace Meredith. Grace? What are you doing here in my driveway holding gazpacho?"

"Oh, just helping out." I tried to make my voice breezy but it came out like the sound a cement mixer makes when they add the stone.

"Meredith? You said your last name was Toffee. I'm confused." Mrs. Herman stood, hands on hips, obviously waiting for an explanation.

"Well, no I didn't. Not really. See, when Toffee introduced himself, you assumed he was my father. He's not." I tried to smile, tried to put a good face on things, but Louise summed it up as—I had learned in such a short time—only she could.

"You lied." She let go of her side of the heavy plastic bowl and stalked to the van. I scrambled to hang on and sat down hard in the dirt.

The sound of car tires crunching on the lane caught Sybil and Lindsey's attention. "OK, I don't know what's going on here but I have a party to cater and I need all the help I can get. Grace, I hired you to do a job and you're going to do it. We can sort this all out later."

16. it's only rock and roll

working lindsey and her friend Rick's party was more uncomfortable for me than walking down a red carpet through hoards of photographers while wearing two-inch heels and a tight skirt. Mrs. Herman kept things moving like the professional she was, but I dreaded having to explain my lie when the party ended.

Louise pretty much ignored me except to hiss and narrow her eyes. Since there was no longer a reason to keep where I lived a secret, I did take Sybil up on her offer to drive me home at least partway.

"You can drop me at the carousel. I'll walk from there. I'm really very sorry about the misunderstanding tonight. It's just that it's hard sometimes being the daughter of a celebrity. Everyone wants a piece of Constance and she tries to keep me out of the limelight. I just wanted to be anonymous for once."

"Yeah, boo hoo, poor little rich girl," said Louise.

"Here's what you earned tonight for helping out, Grace." Mrs. Herman counted out some bills and handed them to me. "You were a big help," she said. "You can drop off the uniform and pick up your clothes tomorrow."

My feet were sore and my arms ached from carrying heavy trays, but what hurt most was the loss of a friend. Even one I'd had for such a short time. That night I didn't find the Chinese lanterns charming. As I approached my new temporary home, I spotted an SUV like the one that had almost squashed Louise and me the day before. Unbidden, part of a song lyric leaped into my head: "Sometimes you're the windshield, sometimes you're the bug." I almost wished I'd been the bug before I had the chance to disappoint everyone so much.

What had Louise said that driver's name was? Mike something? My footsteps crunched on the gravel path as the screen door swung open, throwing a rectangle of light onto the porch steps.

Intuition told me this was not a good time to be observed, so I ducked behind a shrub at the corner of the house.

"Look, Connie, we just wanted to know if she was with you. We have a right to see her, you know." A man's voice, deep but a little whiney, floated out into the humid night.

"Number one, don't call me Connie. Those days are

over. It's Constance. Number two, you have no rights when it comes to Grace. If you come back here or try to contact her, I will call the police. Do you understand?"

My head spun. This man wanted to see me. Had a right to see me? Why? What was this all about? A thought hit me between the eyes like a stone. Was this guy my father?

"We'll fight this, Connie. You haven't heard the last of us." Heavy footsteps pounded down the wooden risers. I rose from my hiding place.

"Hey!" I walked into the light just as the man turned around. His face was in shadow, but I had seen it clearly the day before, snarling from the driver's seat.

"Grace, stop!" Constance ran down the steps and put herself between this Mike person and me. She turned to him. "Mike, we aren't alone here, and if you take another step there will be consequences." He hesitated, then, without another word, opened the SUV door, climbed in, and clunked it closed. The engine roared to life and he pulled away, spraying gravel.

My entire body was strung like a tightrope. Sore feet and aching arms forgotten, I faced my mother. "Who was that?"

"Not now, Grace." Constance, despite her tough talk, looked visibly shaken. Even in the dimness of the porch light I could see she was trembling, and little beads of perspiration had broken out on her forehead.

"Now is as good a time as any, Mother." The emotions of the last two days crashed down on me, coupled with the ache around my heart I had become so accustomed to.

The door opened. "Are you two OK?" It was Camilla's voice but I knew Toffee lurked just out of sight.

I whirled on her. "And what do *you* know about it?"

Camilla continued talking while Constance moved quietly up the stairs and disappeared into the house like a ghost. "Everything will become clear with time."

I snorted. "Where did you get that line, a fortune cookie?"

I pushed past Camilla, stormed into the house, and stomped up the stairs. I slammed the door to my room twice for good measure and threw myself on the bed.

I clutched Froggy and cried. The door opened but I didn't lift my head. Someone sat on the edge of the bed; I felt the mattress give under them. The sobs gushed out of me like geysers.

A hand touched my back. I shrugged, trying to throw it off, but it stayed and rubbed in small circles until the geysers had slowed to a trickle.

"Grace, I'm sorry. I have something I want to share with you, and I shouldn't have gone off to New York without doing it." Constance sounded as wiped out as I felt. I sat up and turned around. The box sat on the dressing table.

"You never did find the key, did you, Gracie?"

"It's Grace. The Gracie days are over." Constance winced at my words then smiled wanly and opened the dressing table drawer.

"Whatever you want, Grace."

She took out the lipstick tube and removed the top. "What would I save a lipstick for all this time? This tube was old before I graduated from high school, but it came in handy." She turned the tube over and tapped it twice on the table. The dried-up cotton-candy-pink cylinder dropped out into her hand followed by a small key. She placed the key in the lock and turned it. I realized I was holding my breath.

We sat side by side on the bed. Constance lifted the lid. I peered in and let out my breath. What a jumble of stuff! Not at all like the Constance I thought I knew. A musty odor rose from the chaos I saw. Constance reached in and pushed aside some papers—were they yellowed photographs? I craned my neck to see, and my heart thudded in anticipation of finally being able to put a face and a name to the man I knew only as my father. Constance pulled out a ring, not a picture. A guy's ring. It was wrapped with yarn. She held it up and turned it back and forth before slipping it on her left ring finger.

"This was your father's high school ring. Girls used to wrap their boyfriend's rings with yarn to make them fit. I never got a chance to give it back to him. I don't think he would have taken it back anyway. He's a stubborn one. You get a little of that from him, Grace."

"What else do I get from him?" We were maintaining a delicate emotional balance. Constance had had a plan to tell me about my father. But I had a feeling that the SUV guy's visit had not been part of the plan. She took a deep breath and carried on.

"Your father came from an old island family. They lived Up Island, which is the other end of the island from here. He used to have to hitchhike to visit me or borrow his mother's car. He was very handsome. You look a lot like him, Grace. Especially around the eyes. Most of the Suttons have those deep blue eyes."

Sutton! That was the SUV guy's last name. I wracked my brain to remember if his eyes were like my eyes, but all I could dredge up was his voice when he yelled at us to watch where we were going. "That idiot" was what Louise had called him. Had he come here tonight for me? I thought about the conversation that I had overheard when I arrived home. Constance didn't know how long I'd been crouching in the bushes. Maybe it was time to fess up.

"I heard . . ."

"Constance? Hey Constance, you in there?" A woman's voice called from the front porch, followed by knocking.

"Who could that be at this hour?" Constance sighed and closed the box.

"I know who it is. It's Lindsey. The second party we catered tonight was hers. She wondered where you were. . . ."

"Grace, the things in this box are precious to me. I want to tell you about your father properly. I know I've taken a long time. I know now how much it means to you. I've been selfish. I thought our little family was enough. Sometimes, between people, it takes a long time to get over the disappointment they can cause each other." Constance looked at me, willing me with her eyes to understand. She put the ring back in the box, closed it with a click, and stood, slipping the tiny key into her pocket. "I have to go downstairs. I hope you understand."

Molten lava bubbled under my ribs. My hands ached to grab the box from her and run. "I know all about disappointment, *Mother.*" I practically spit the words at her. "Go see your friend. Don't worry about me. I'll be fine."

it was close to midnight. Louise had said the club was near the ferry landing. I was pretty sure I could find that. I listened for voices. Constance and Lindsey started in the foyer and moved to the kitchen.

"Where's Rick tonight?" Inquiring Minds wanted to know.

"Oh, he's at a little rock club down on the beach. I just walked up to say hi."

"I'm happy to see you, but how did you know where to find me?" Constance sounded genuinely puzzled.

"Honey, everyone on the island knows where to find you. I just asked the bouncer at the club and he gave me perfect directions."

Camilla was sleeping and I assumed Toffee had shut himself away in the den to read. In bare feet, flip-flops in hand, I took each step slowly and froze when the third from the bottom creaked. No one seemed to notice. I crept across the foyer, pushed open the screen door, and closed it silently behind me.

17. coming clean

i heard the band before I saw the club. They were jamming away on an old Led Zeppelin song. The club sat near the ferry landing across the road on the beach, nothing more than a ramshackle building with a tin roof. A line snaked from the front door out along the sand. A big guy wearing jeans and a tank top seemed to be in charge of who got in and who didn't. I was very familiar with this tactic. Constance always got in. The Constance wannabes didn't. I slid along the line looking for Louise. I didn't know if she would talk to me, but I really wanted to try to explain myself again. I hadn't been honest with her, just like Constance hadn't been honest with me, and I knew how it felt to be on the receiving end of that.

I spotted her not in line but slouched against the building. When she saw me approaching, she didn't walk off. I took that as a good sign. I leaned up against the building next to her.

"Hey."

"Yeah, whatever."

I tried again. "Why aren't you inside? It sounds like a good band."

Louise stared at me for a second, sighed, and decided to talk to me. "It's a great band but they won't let minors in, and I don't have a fake ID like some of the rest of these losers." She tossed her head toward the line.

"Me either. Constance would kill me."

"My mother would kill me if she knew I was even here. Hey, want to take a walk? This is lame." Louise pushed off the building and I did the same. We walked along the beach in silence for a while.

"So, you're really Constance Meredith's daughter, huh? Why didn't you tell me?"

"Well, some people just get to know me to get close to Constance. Besides, you have that celebrity sighting column and all. I just wasn't sure I could trust you."

Louise was quiet for a long time. "Did you really like my room or did you think it was lame?"

"Are you kidding? Your room is totally awesome. Wait until you see my room. Talk about lame. It's like from the sixties or something."

"You mean I can come to your house? Really?"

"Yeah, sure. And if it's OK with Constance, you can probably officially write her up as being sighted. We're supposed to be going to the beach tomorrow. Want to come?" I figured if Louise was there, I wouldn't have to talk too much with Constance, and I might actually have a good time.

"Why do you call her Constance instead of Mom?"

I had never talked about this with anyone. Maybe if I shared it with Louise, she would see that I really did trust her.

"I've never told anybody before, but I guess it's just that when I was growing up, I heard everyone else calling her Constance so I did, too. I guess she thought I would eventually stop, but I never did. It's been Constance and Toffee and Camilla—you'll meet her tomorrow—and me for as long as I can remember. Sometimes it's almost as if Constance and I are more like friends than mother and daughter. I know most kids don't call their mothers by their first names, but it makes some kind of weird sense with us. I mean she's the adult, but, it's . . ." My words trailed off and the only sound was the distant rhythm of the band and the waves breaking on the shore. "It's hard to explain."

"It's cool. My mother would have a cow if I ever called her Sybil to her face. Listen, I think I'm going to go home. What time tomorrow?"

"Around nine, I guess. Do you know which house?"

"Grace, in case you haven't figured it out yet, everyone on the island knows which house. Later."

18. the beach

when i arrived home the house was dark. The lanterns and porch light had been extinguished. I hoped the door was unlocked. I climbed the steps and was reaching for the screen door when a figure stepped out of the shadows. "Jeez!"

"Relax. Grace. It's only me." Constance's voice.

"Um, I was, well, I mean . . ."

"Save it. As soon as I heard there was a rock club nearby I knew you'd try to hear the band. I did the same thing when I was your age. Tell me, were they any good?"

I expelled the breath I'd been holding. She didn't sound mad. That was a good thing.

"Yeah, from what I could hear from the outside. I couldn't get in because I'm underage."

"Well, I'm relieved to know you don't have fake ID like

I did. Let's go in. It's late and I have a big day planned tomorrow." She put one arm around my shoulders and pulled open the door with her free hand.

"Really?"

"Really what?"

"You had fake ID?"

"Yes, but it isn't something I'm proud of."

I yawned. "Say good night, Constance." My anger had disappeared—for the moment I was happy to have a mother who cared enough to wait up and worry about me.

"Good night, Gracie. Grace, that is. By the way, I like your hair. And your earrings match your eyes. Just don't get anything else pierced without talking to me first, OK?"

We climbed the stairs in silence. I fell into bed exhausted, but feeling better than I had in a while.

the next morning dawned sunny and clear. I still hadn't unpacked and was running out of options for clean, cool outfits. I decided on a pair of black denim shorts over my red one-piece bathing suit and the same flip-flops as yesterday. I glanced in the mirror, brushed my new hair, turned my new earrings, and, for once, was happy with what I saw.

Something smelled good in the direction of the kitchen. Breakfast, the most important meal of the day, according to Toffee. Well, who was I to argue? I pushed open the kitchen door.

"Good morning, Grace. French toast today." Toffee set a plate and the maple syrup in front of me. "Dig in." Constance sat at the table looking perfect as usual as she nibbled on a piece of dry toast and sipped herbal tea. Obviously, she hadn't gotten the memo about breakfast being so important.

"Where's Camilla?" I asked.

"Oh, probably upstairs deciding which T-shirt goes best with her bathing suit," said Toffee. He plopped three pieces of battered bread into the skillet. They sputtered and popped. Someone knocked at the door.

"Anybody home?" It was Louise.

"Come on in. We're in the kitchen," I called. I took a bite of French toast and gave Toffee the thumbs-up.

"Hey." Louise pushed open the door, and once again I was immediately made aware of my hastily chosen outfit. Suddenly my one-piece Speedo didn't pack much of a punch. This girl oozed style.

"So this is Louise." My mother, always the star, stood and took Louise's hand in hers. Constance never shakes hands; she simply holds a person's hand in hers while she looks them directly in the eyes. "How do you like living on the island, Louise?"

"Oh, um, it's OK, I guess." Louise's cool seemed to have

abandoned her and left her tongue-tied. It was a common reaction around my mother. Sometimes people just don't know what to say. I jumped in.

"Louise wants to be a journalist. Maybe you could give her an interview while we're here."

My mother tossed her blond mane and smiled. "Of course. It will be a welcome relief from the press I usually deal with."

"Thank you, Miss Meredith."

"Call me Constance. Everyone does."

"Hey, want some French toast?" I asked. "Toffee makes the best there is."

For the first time Louise seemed to notice there were other people on the planet besides my mother. "Oh, hi. Nice to see you again. That looks great but no, I had a protein shake. I'm good."

"A protein shake. You and Camilla will be exchanging recipes by the end of the day. Don't tell me you're a vegan, too." Toffee laughed and began running water in the sink.

"Leave the dishes. It's too nice to spend another moment inside. Grace, get your stuff together and don't forget sunscreen. You know how you burn."

we dragged beach chairs, towels, boogie boards, and other paraphernalia from the Jeep to the beach, where

I know I would have been happy to deposit it, slather on SPF 300, and plop down. Constance had other ideas.

"Let's walk just a little farther down the beach and get away from the crowd." She wore huge sunglasses and a straw hat with a wide brim. She might as well have had on a name tag for all the protection from fans they gave her. We stopped at least five times on our trek up the beach for her to sign autographs, and we never did get away from the crowd—only the crowd with bathing suits.

"You really don't want to go much farther. Nude bathing is optional at this end of the beach," Louise said. But Constance was sidetracked by her public and didn't stop until we were faced with a mixed nude beach volleyball game in our path. Naked and volleyball don't mix. Trust me. The body parts that flap and jiggle just looked painful to me. And if you think sand in your bathing suit is annoying, just imagine where it might find itself when you're naked and lunging for game point, only to end up facedown on the beach. It took me all day to shut out that mental picture.

"A plastic surgeon could make a bundle around here," muttered Toffee, who prided himself on keeping in shape.

When we finally got settled, I suggested that Louise and I go for a walk. It was the only way we could put enough distance between us and the adults to talk privately, and I had questions that I hoped she might be able to answer. Besides, I'd seen some cute boys I thought we could check out.

"Oh, swell. There's my *favorite* person," said Louise. A girl's shrill laugh drew my attention to a group of teenagers reclining on beach towels a little ways away. In the middle, commanding the center of attention and wearing perhaps the smallest bikini I had ever seen, was Tanya Sutton. Suddenly, an epiphany hit me like a stone between the eyes. I'd been so busy obsessing about Mike Sutton maybe being my father that I'd totally blanked on the fact he had a daughter. My half sister? I watched her flirt with the boys who flocked around her—throwing sand, screaming when one of them picked her up and took a few threatening steps toward the water. Well, one thing was for sure: even if we shared a father, we were nothing alike.

"Hey, earth to Grace, let's get out of here. I've had about all I can take of the Tanya Sutton Show." Louise pulled my arm to get me moving, but it was too late.

"Well, if it isn't Herman and her new little friend." Tanya strode through the sand toward us. A blond amazon. The boys trailed in her wake like abandoned puppies. "Aren't you going to introduce me?"

"She doesn't want to meet you, Tanya. Go back and play with your groupies." Louise flipped her hair and turned to walk away.

"I'm Grace Meredith. Constance Meredith is my

mother." I looked for any recognition from Tanya—a flicker that she might know more than I did.

"Oh yeah, the movie star? My dad used to have the hots for her in high school. His friends tease him about it all the time. Especially when they've been into the Jack Daniel's." She dug a toe into the sand. With each breath, her chest threatened to escape the scraps of cloth covering it. "Constance Meredith's daughter, huh? I'm not impressed." She turned on her heel and walked away. The boys followed but I caught two of them looking back at us.

"She is *totally* jealous of you. I love it!" Louise was practically dancing with glee.

"What are you talking about? She walked away. She looked at me like I was a pair of size-twelve jeans that somehow found their way into her size-zero closet."

"Tanya likes to be the center of attention. You are the daughter of a big star. Of course that threatens her. And, I saw Tony and Andy giving you the eye. I wish Amanda and Syndi were here. They would love this turn of events, Tanya not being the only show in town."

"Who?"

"A couple of my good friends. They're both gone for the summer—until the first week in August."

I suppressed a flicker of jealousy. Of course Louise had other friends. She hadn't been sitting around in a vacuum waiting for me to show up.

"Look, there's something I have to ask you, but you can't tell anyone." We sank down into the wet sand near the shoreline, out of earshot of Tanya and her minions. "What do you know about Mike Sutton besides that he's a lousy driver and that Tanya is his daughter?"

"Why?" Louise's green eyes met mine. I hesitated. This was a big deal. Not only might her answer tell me something that might confirm to me he was my father, but also how I handled it would affect Constance's privacy. How she had kept his identity a secret until now I couldn't guess, but few people knew she had an ailing father in a nursing home, either, so she had her ways.

"Well, I don't know who my father is. Last night when I got back home I heard Constance arguing with Mike Sutton and most of the argument was about me."

"Oh my God. You think he's your father? Yuck, no offense. I don't know too much more. They live at the other end of the island. Tanya is sixteen and she has her own car, which is why she's always down here. It's pretty dead up there. Not much going on."

"OK, so Tanya is a year older than I am. That doesn't prove anything. Do you think your mother might know something?" As I talked I dug my fingers into the sand until the hole filled up with water.

"Probably, but she's gone to Boston today. Why don't you just ask your own mother?"

I explained to Louise about Constance's plan, her determination to keep the truth about my father from me until she thought I was old enough to understand.

"Maybe she's protecting you from something. Maybe she's protecting you from him." Her tone of voice caught my attention. She stared out into the ocean.

"What is it? What's wrong?"

"Look, you haven't seen a father figure around my house, have you? My mother threw him out a few years ago. Let's just say it's better that way. Mike Sutton is a drunk. If he is your father, I feel sorry for you. But if you want to find out, I'll help you."

I told Louise about the box and Constance's promise to go through it with me. "If she does that like she says she will, I'll have all the answers I need."

"Here's hoping you get your answers and one of them isn't Tanya Sutton. I can't imagine having to deal with her for the rest of my life."

The rest of the day flew by. Louise taught me how to bodysurf and I taught her how to use a boogie board. Constance slathered us with sunscreen whenever we got near her. Toffee relaxed under a beach umbrella with a book.

We had dinner at The Black Dog, and then dropped Louise off just as the lanterns in the campgrounds began to twinkle on.

19. investigations

sleep didn't come easily that night. Even after a shower I had sand in places I didn't want to think about, and despite Constance's vigilance with the sunscreen my shoulders had burned. At two in the morning I headed downstairs to get a drink of water and noticed a light on in Constance's room. If she couldn't sleep, either, I reasoned, then maybe we could talk some more. But when I came back up, her room was dark.

Louise called the next morning. The phone woke me and I grabbed it and flopped back into bed.

"Sybil grounded me for a week. She heard I was at the club. News travels fast on this little rock."

"Bummer. My mother didn't say much at all except that she did the same thing, sneaking out, when she was my age," I said to Louise.

"Yeah, well Sybil isn't exactly the rock club type. More like the garden club type. Gotta go—if she catches me on the phone, she'll make it two weeks. Grounding is absolutely medieval."

I hung up. My stomach rumbled and I headed down for breakfast. As I pushed open the kitchen door, Constance was telling Camilla and Toffee about her plans for the next few days.

"So, after lunch at Lindsey's today I'm meeting some old friends for dinner." She paused to sip her herbal tea. "Then, tomorrow I have a Campground Association meeting and I'm going sailing and later in the week . . ."

Her mouth continued to move but I tuned her out. So much for the mother-daughter time I had envisioned. Constance was obviously busy establishing herself back on Martha's Vineyard.

"Earth to Grace. I asked you if you wanted to go to Edgartown with me on Thursday. They have some wonderful restaurants there. We could have lunch, just the two of us."

You're penciling me in for Thursday? How nice of you, Constance, I thought. What I said was, "I'm pretty busy this week, too, Constance, so if you don't mind, I don't think so. Maybe another time." Two could play this game. Despite the disappointment that pressed against my heart, I was determined not to make a scene. I swallowed hard and dug into a bowl of granola that might as well have been sawdust for all the flavor I could taste. "Yummy." I smiled in Toffee's direction, ignoring the puzzled look on Constance's face.

She had failed me for the last time. I would find out about my father without her. I choked down the last spoonful of cereal around the growing lump in my throat. I scraped back my chair. "Well, I have a busy day, I'll see you all later." When I reached the privacy of my room the tears came. I buried my face in my pillow. I wouldn't give Constance the satisfaction of hearing me cry again. When the waterworks stopped I pulled on my clothes, ran a brush through my hair, and headed down the stairs and out the front door.

I wandered around the ferry landing hoping, unreasonably, that my dark mood would spread to the happy vacationers around me, but I was invisible to them. Finally, I walked to the carousel building, went in, and slouched against one of the arcade games in what I hoped was a passable Louise imitation. I watched people from behind my dark sunglasses and fingered the brass ring in my pocket. I was still carrying it with me faithfully, for all the good it had done me. I pulled it out, thinking I might as well use it for the free ride, when a little kid bumped into me and the ring went flying.

I decided that if I saw it on the floor in plain sight I

would get it. If not, it was history. It winked at me from about two feet away. I bent and picked it up. As I turned around, something hanging above and half behind the game I had been leaning against caught my eye. It was the album cover Louise had told me about. Flying Horses the band riding Flying Horses the carousel. There was a pay phone in the carousel building. I dropped in some change and called Louise. It rang and rang and rang but I knew she was there. Finally, she came on the line.

"Hello?"

"You sound out of breath," I said.

"Yeah, well we don't all have phones in our rooms, you know. What's up? Make it fast; Sybil is in the garden cutting herbs. She'll be back in soon."

"I'm at the carousel and I was looking at the Flying Horses album cover."

"Yeah, what about it? I thought you weren't a fan."

"Well, I wasn't until you told me more about them. Now I'm curious." Curious—and I wanted to know all there was to know about the island my mother had lived on. Maybe she had known this band, heard them play even, before they got famous. "I know the band was named after the carousel and Henry L, the lead singer, got his stage name from the horse you always ride. What else is there?"

"Did you notice they paint their faces like carousel horses?"

"They do?"

"When you get off the phone, look at the cover again then go look at Henry L the horse. Henry L paints his face for concerts the same way the horse is painted."

"I'll do that, thanks."

"I gotta go. The warden is coming."

I hung up and took another look at the album cover. The glass covering it was dusty and fly-specked. Not too many people interested in the history of Flying Horses anymore, I guessed.

I bought a ticket and, when the carousel stopped, found Henry L and climbed on. I studied his face. The eyes were deep blue, almost violet. A black blaze ran down his nose. The painted bridle was green and brown with touches of red and gold. The carousel started up, and as it whirled faster and faster so did my mind. The thought of Mike Sutton turning out to be my father, the man I had thought about all these years, romanticized, made larger than life, made me think about never eating again. The carousel music tinkled behind me as I headed for home thinking about what I knew. And what I didn't.

20. up island

by the time Louise was done being grounded I had a plan. Constance wasn't the only one who could make plans. I had been a model teenager for a week. I politely said no to every outing Constance suggested.

"No, thank you, Constance, you go ahead with your friends to the Cape," is what I said. *I have things to find out and I can't find them out while I'm being the perfect daughter for your friends,* is what I thought.

I helped Toffee with shopping and meals and went on a short field trip. "Yes, Toffee. The walking tour of Edgartown was fascinating," is what I said. But *Blah, blah, blah,* is what I thought.

I gave Camilla fashion tips. "I think the red Black Dog shirt really brings out the highlights in your hair," is what I said. *Enough with the dang T-shirts, already,* is what I thought.

I finally unpacked my clothes and lugged them to the basement to do my own wash.

On the first day she could get out of the house, I met Louise in front of The Beauty Barn. "Is your mother home? I think she might be able to help me."

Louise shrugged. "No, she's catering a luncheon today, and boy am I glad that Carole is feeling better or I would have been roped into helping. Why? What do you think my mother knows?"

"I know Mike Sutton has something to do with this, and my mother said I have the Sutton eyes. I want to know what your mother thinks that means."

Louise thought for a long minute. "Come with me." I went back to her house with her where she rummaged around in the bookcase in the living room.

"What are you doing?"

"When you're a journalist you have to learn to investigate, to go to more than one source. Tada!" She pulled a book from the bottom shelf and blew the dust from the cover.

"I don't get it."

"It's a yearbook. If Mike Sutton went to high school with our mothers, then he'll be in here."

"Way to go. But this is an old yearbook. The pictures will be black and white. Pretty hard to tell eye color from that."

"Maybe there will be a picture of him with your mother. Maybe they were, like, class couple or prom king and queen or something." She sat down on the couch and began flipping pages. There was Constance smiling out over the years, looking gorgeous even as a teenager.

"Wait, here's the prom court. Isn't that your mother?"

My eyes searched the picture and found her familiar face. "She's wearing the dress I found in my closet. She told me she went to the prom with my father, that it was the last night they were really happy together." I squinted at the grainy picture. The photographer hadn't done a very good job. The boy next to my mother was only half in the picture. The rest of him had been poorly edited out. My heart sank and tears formed, ready to fall. The picture had been labeled only "Prom Court." There were no names to identify the people in it. I peered harder; it was impossible to tell eye color. I couldn't be sure it was Mike Sutton. Too much of him was missing and too many years had passed to say for sure who the young man with his arm around my mother was.

"I need to get Up Island. I need to talk to the Suttons, and I need to do it today."

"Can you ride a bike?" Louise looked at me and smiled.

"Yeah, I have a mountain bike at home."

"Well, you can ride my mom's bike and I'll take mine, but we have to be back before she is or she'll have a fit. I'm not supposed to go Up Island without permission."

A few minutes later we were on the main road heading to the other end of the island. Louise pedaled evenly beside me. I switched gears and tried to look as effortlessly cool as she did. Soon we were out of the business of Oak Bluffs.

I was charmed by the rolling landscape, meadows, and stone walls. I guess Toffee had trained my sense of observation a little bit. This part of the island was different from the one we had just left. It seemed more peaceful, less crowded. No mopeds in sight.

"This is really pretty."

Louise glanced in my direction. "You wouldn't think so if you rode the same route in the Loser Cruiser every day." She turned her attention to the road again.

"What's a Loser Cruiser?"

"I forgot you live on Planet Hollywood. Loser Cruiser, also known as the Big Cheese, is the school bus."

"Why do you ride it?"

Louise turned to me and pulled down her sunglasses. "Because it's the only way to get to school. Sybil won't drive me, so I have to ride the bus. But next year, when I get my license, I'm getting a car. I've been saving up. Is Constance going to buy you a car for your sixteenth birthday?" A tone had crept into her voice, almost a challenge.

"I've never really thought about it, I guess. We're not home enough for me to get much use out of a car."

Louise pushed her shades back up and sped up a little.

End of discussion. We pedaled in silence for a while until Louise stopped.

"Well, here we are. The house is about a quarter mile down that lane." I looked at the narrow gravel and dirt lane bordered on each side by a tumbling-down stone wall and overgrown underbrush. Were my answers at the end of that lane?

21. the suttons

we started up the lane. The gravel made it harder to pedal. Some sort of bug seemed to be attracted to the sweat building up around my hairline. The sun had ducked behind a cloud, but the heat and humidity had gotten worse. Constance would freak out if she knew where I was, biking up the dusty road to her old boyfriend's house in search of answers. Guilt pricked me like the pins and needles you feel when your foot has gone to sleep. Nobody knew where we were. I flashed back on Mike Sutton's angry face as he looked at us out of his SUV window. Was I leading Louise into trouble? This was my battle, not hers.

"Let's ditch the bikes and walk. This gravel is a pain." Louise stopped, got off, and walked her bike to the side of the lane. "Behind this bush should be good."

We hid the bikes and continued on foot.

"Hang on a sec." Louise stopped and dug around in her jeans pocket until she pulled out a hair tie. She bent at the waist, flipped her hair over her head, and wound it up in a knot. "Man, it's hot. Days like this make me want to shave my head. Maybe Marcy would tattoo it for me." She grinned.

I grinned back. "Look, you don't have to do this with me. I don't know what I'm going to find out when I get there."

Louise suddenly pushed me into a prickly bush and hissed at me to get down and be quiet. Then I heard what she'd heard—gravel crunching under tires coming our way, fast. The SUV passed our hiding place in a cloud of dust heading for the main road.

"That was Mike Sutton's car. We came all this way for nothing." Louise stood up and brushed off her jeans. "Now we have to ride all the way back to town."

"What do you mean came all this way for nothing? I want to look him in the face when I ask him if he's my father, and I'll wait all day to do it if I have to. Let's go." I walked right out of my trendy flip-flops trying to navigate the underbrush and had to stop to retrieve them. I threw them out onto the gravel and stepped carefully into them one at a time. Louise had turned and was looking at me with her head tipped to the side. "Well, are you coming?" I demanded.

She sighed and pushed some stray hairs behind her ears. "Let's get this over with. I just hope Tanya isn't there," she muttered.

"What's the deal with you two?"

"Look, she's one of 'The Populars' and I'm most certainly not. My family doesn't have waterfront property or a daddy that buys them everything. Tanya has everything. She's gorgeous and can get any guy she wants. You have everything. You don't know how real people live. You probably are sisters. She got the body and the father and you got the movie star life." Louise turned away after she spit those words at me. I touched her arm, but she pulled away.

"Look, you're right. I've never been in a house like yours, with a normal mother who has a normal job. I don't know what it's like to Fake and Bake or ride a Loser Cruiser, and until a couple of weeks ago I'd never been on a carousel or tasted cotton candy. You think I have it made and you probably wouldn't believe it if I told you I think you have it made. But I do. I need your help. I would never have gotten this far without you."

Louise turned around, sunglasses in place, and studied me. "Well, that's true. Besides, Tanya did steal my boyfriend. The one thing I had that she didn't. To her he was just another guy, but not to me. Getting dumped for Tanya hurt. It hurt a lot."

Since I had never had a boyfriend, I didn't know how to respond to that. I gave her a sympathetic look and we trudged along in silence for a while. I reminded myself to always wear sensible shoes in the future. My feet were killing me.

"There it is," said Louise.

"There's Tanya." I shaded my eyes to get a better look at my potential half sister. She was sitting in a lawn chair wearing a tangerine bikini that was a perfect complement to her tanned skin.

"Let's go knock on the door. Might as well get this ball rolling," said Louise. The grass felt cool under my feet. As we passed the garage, I noticed the door was ajar, and inside was a rusted station wagon. On the left rear bumper was a bumper sticker. GRACE HAPPENS was spelled out in faded blue and yellow letters. I felt the blood drain from my head and would have fallen if Louise hadn't seen me sway and grabbed me.

"Are you OK?"

I pointed to the garage. She peered in and I watched as her eyes moved over the bumper sticker. She turned back to me. "I think we've come to the right place."

"Well, hello. Is there something I can do for you girls?" The soft voice came from behind me. I turned and looked into a pair of blue eyes. Just like my own.

"Oh, I'm sorry, ma'am, we were just admiring your

bumper sticker." The woman was elderly, maybe in her sixties or seventies, but it was hard to tell. A cloud of white hair swirled around her head, and her face was tanned and covered in a net of fine lines. But her eyes twinkled.

"You look a little pale. Come on into the house and sit down. I just made a pitcher of lemonade. That will fix you right up. Are you two friends of my granddaughter, Tanya? You look about her age."

"I go to school with Tanya," said Louise.

"I'm sure she would like to join us. Would you mind running down to the beach to get her?"

Louise hesitated and I shot her a look. "Sure, no problem," she finally said.

We followed a path past the garage. The roof sagged over walls sporting peeling white paint. The rusted station wagon crouched inside, its bumper sticker barely visible in the shadows. We had reached the house. She opened the screen door and held it for me to pass through first. I found myself in a small, spotless kitchen. My brain was a swirl of emotions. I knew this soft-spoken woman puttering around her kitchen, retrieving lemonade from the refrigerator and four glasses from a cupboard, had all the answers.

"Go on into the living room and make yourself comfortable. I'll put some sugar cookies on a plate and be right in."

The overstuffed couch in the cozy room looked

inviting, but I was drawn to the room beyond. It was a music room and sported a piano next to a modern key-board and drum set.

"Here you go. Help yourself. You still look a little green around the gills," she said, setting a tray with two glasses and a plate of cookies on a small table inside the door.

I took a deep swallow from the icy glass and was about to ask who the musician in the family was when I heard yelling coming from outside.

She peered out the window.

"Oh dear. It looks like Tanya and your friend are argu-ing. I think I'd better get out there. I'll take them some lemonade and cookies. A snack is just the thing, I think. What did you say your friend's name was?"

Raised voices drifted through the open window with the breeze that blew the white gauzy curtains and scattered papers from a music stand.

"Her name is Louise. I hope we haven't caused any trouble by coming here."

She stopped in the doorway and smiled at me. "Grace, I've been waiting for you for a long time. You're no trouble at all."

Although it was warm in the house, a chill climbed up my spine. Camilla would have understood. "You know who I am?"

"I knew the minute I looked into your eyes. It was like

looking into a mirror. You have my eyes, Grace, and your father's. We'll talk more after I settle the battle outside." She turned away and I heard the screen door slam. I glanced out the window to see her wading through the overgrown lawn toward Louise and Tanya. They ignored her and, while their voices had faded, they continued to gesture at each other. My time was short. I knelt and gathered the papers on the floor into a pile. My eye was drawn to something familiar propped between the piano and the wall. I put the sheet music back on the music stand and dropped back to my knees. It was a framed album cover: Flying Horses the band riding Flying Horses the carousel.

22. windows of the soul

"get off my property. Don't you have anything better to do than harass me?"

"Oh, what is your issue, Tanya? I'd go out of my way to avoid you. I have my reasons for being here and they don't include you." It sounded like a regular catfight.

Still holding the framed album cover, I looked out the window. Tanya had gotten off the lounge chair and was facing Louise, who stood, hands on hips, chin jutting out. While I couldn't see her eyes, I had come to know her well enough to imagine the sparks flying from them.

"Maybe I'm not as popular as you, Tanya, but at least I'm not a boyfriend stealer."

"Billy came along pretty willingly, Herman."

"Oh, yeah? He may have gone willingly, but he sure didn't stick around very long, did he?"

Tanya turned and stalked off toward the ocean.

"Tanya," my grandmother called. But she didn't go after her. Instead she set the tray on a stump and hurried up a path that seemed to lead from the lawn around to the front of the house. Louise turned and scanned the back of the house, clearly looking for me. I stared once more at the album cover, at the Sutton eyes peering out from the scarlet face paint that surrounded them. Henry L was my father. My gut told me so. But who was Henry L?

"What's going on here?" Mike Sutton's voice rang out over the yard. I hadn't heard him come back, but that was OK. I had a few questions for Mike Sutton.

I pushed open the screen door and steeled myself for the conversation I thought was coming. As I walked toward the beach I reminded myself that I had not come this far to leave without answers. I walked through the grass toward the little group at the edge of the yard. Mike Sutton's voice was a faint rumble over the waves breaking on the beach. Tanya stood facing the water, her back to everyone. Louise was closing the distance between us like a heat-seeking missile.

"We need to get out of here. Mike is being his usual charming self, Mrs. Sutton is trying to hold it together with cookies and lemonade, and I've had about all of Tanya's garbage I'm going to take. Let's go."

"No, I've come this far and I'm going to find out

everything I can. Mrs. Sutton is my grandmother. She practically told me so herself. You can go or stay, but I wish you'd stay." It was time to get some answers.

"OK, but if Tanya says one more syllable to me I'm going to deck her."

Mike Sutton made a production of watching us approach. He bowed deeply. I decided then and there that if he really was my father I would never call him Dad. Another chill ran up my spine and directly into my head, feeling like the brain freeze the slush at the carousel had given me. I resisted the urge to put my fingers to the top of my nose a la Constance.

"Well, Grace. It's a pleasure to finally meet you." He held out his hand. I crossed my arms across my chest.

"Are you my father?" There, the question had been asked. My heart thudded so loudly in my ears, I wondered if I would actually be able to hear his answer.

Mike Sutton removed his Oakleys, revealing hazel eyes. "Not that I didn't try. Your mother caught my attention the first day she walked down the hall to her locker, but I didn't stand a chance against my brother."

My heart beat so hard now that I thought everyone could hear it, and the lemonade I had gulped a few minutes earlier threatened to make an unannounced appearance, but I stood my ground. Constance says I can be stubborn, and I guess she's right.

"Where is he?"

"Your father? Well, he's certainly not here." Mike put the shades back on. "He does take good care of us, though. Oh yes, my brother, Robert, has done well for himself."

23. family reunion

robert sutton was my father. Finally, I had a name.
"My father has done well at what?" I needed my suspi-
cions that Henry L and Robert Sutton were one and the
same confirmed. After all, there could be other brothers.
The guy on the album cover might not be who I thought
he was even if we did have the same eyes. My father
could be a very successful international banker or lawyer
or something.

"Obviously you aren't a fan," said Mike. "Your father
is the one and only Henry L, creator and lead singer of
Flying Horses. A secret he has gone to great lengths to
protect." Mike chuckled. "But I suppose it's OK to tell
you. After all, you found us; it was only a matter of time
before you put the rest of it together, too."

Louise's eyes were as big as saucers. "Oh my God,

Grace! You're Henry L's daughter," she said.

The pounding in my ears had started again. "What do you mean, 'the rest of it'? What else is there? Tell me."

"I think I'll let your mother fill in the blanks," Mike snarled. Then he reached into the pocket of his shorts and pulled out a small silver flask. He twisted off the top, raised it to his lips, and took a hard pull.

"What he's not saying is that if he tells you any more, that generous check that my dear uncle sends each month will stop coming and if that happened we'd be in deep trouble. Right, Dad?" Tanya faced her father. Mike wiped his mouth with the back of his hand and put the flask back in his pocket without answering.

"But why does my father take care of you all? I don't get it."

Tanya opened her mouth to speak just as I noticed a dust cloud moving fast up the dirt road. Constance's Jeep skidded to a stop behind Mike's truck. The driver's-side door opened and out jumped my mother.

"Grace, you're in big trouble!" Constance was visibly upset.

"How did you know I was here?" I asked, confused.

"Your grandmother called me, Grace. If only you could have been patient a little longer, I would have been able to tell you everything. I had it all planned."

The volcano that had been brewing in me since we

arrived on Martha's Vineyard finally erupted.

"You can't plan my life, Mother. And I'm not getting into the Jeep until I have more answers."

"Grace, calm down. I mishandled this, but . . ."

"You can't duck this issue anymore, Constance. I don't need you for answers. I know who my father is and I can find out everything I want to know from him." I swiped at the tears flowing down my face. Constance was silent but I wasn't finished. "Well, *Mother*, what do you think about that? I don't need you or your stupid plans or whatever is in your stupid box."

"If you want to meet your father, you do need her." My grandmother's soft voice cut through my anger like a jet plane through a cloud bank. She stepped up and stood next to Constance, who reached down and took her hand.

"But . . ."

"Your mother knows what she's doing. She knows how to handle your father. Now go along with her." Our eyes met and held. "Believe me, Grace, once you know all the facts you'll understand." My grandmother reached out her free hand to me. I took it and squeezed gently. At that moment, all the fight went out of me.

"When are you planning on telling me the rest?"

Constance took a deep breath. "Your father is not an easy man to track down, but I found him, and he has promised to be on the island tomorrow morning. I think it's best if we wait for him."

Suddenly, my stomach was in free fall. I was going to meet my father. That was what I wanted, right? So why did I feel like I was going to lose my breakfast?

24. grace happens

constance hugged my grandmother, then hustled Louise and me to the Jeep. She put it in reverse and turned around. Near the end of the lane we pulled the bikes out of their hiding place and settled in for the ride back to Oak Bluffs.

No one said very much. My stomach continued to roll at the thought of meeting my father in the morning. I realized I didn't have a clue what he looked like under the face paint.

"Constance, how will I recognize him?"

"He has agreed to come to the house. I'll be there with you. It's been a long time, but I remember what he looks like." Constance gave me a crooked smile before turning her attention to the road.

We stopped at Louise's house first and unloaded the

bikes. Mrs. Herman came outside and thanked Constance for getting us.

"But where were they?" she asked.

"They were Up Island at the Sutton house," Constance replied as her hand drifted to the top of her nose.

Mrs. Herman turned to Louise. "I told you to stay away from that Tanya Sutton. I also told you to be home when I got home."

"But, Mom, we weren't there to see Tanya. Grace was looking for her father."

"Her father?" Mrs. Herman looked at Constance.

"I'm sure Louise will fill you in. Grace and I have some unfinished business at home."

When we got home the house was quiet. Toffee and Camilla were nowhere to be seen.

"I sent them to Boston for a few days."

"Why?" Constance told Camilla everything.

"Grace, it's been important to keep who your father is a secret. I love Camilla and Toffee but, well, you know what a gossip Toffee can be. I just thought it best that the three of us do this alone. Let's see if Toffee left us any dinner."

There were cold cuts and rolls and a salad that only Camilla could have whipped up. My stomach now grumbled instead of rolling. We ate at the kitchen table, and when we finished Constance excused herself to get something from upstairs. I cleared the table, piled the dishes in the sink, and was thinking over the day when Constance pushed open the kitchen door. In her hand was the box I had found under the floor in my room. She put it on the table.

"Sit down, Gracie. Better late than never, huh?"

I pulled a chair up close to hers. She opened the box and reached in.

"This is your father and me senior year. We went to a carnival and they had one of those photo booths where you put in a quarter and get a bunch of pictures." She handed me a narrow strip of photos a little longer than a bookmark. There were maybe a half dozen in all. They clowned and hugged and kissed for the camera. For the first time, I knew that I had his nose as well as his eyes. I studied his face, trying to memorize it. Also, I realized, trying to decide if I had ever seen it before. If he had ever walked into my life. No, this man was a stranger. A stranger I looked like.

Constance rummaged in the box again and came up with the ring I had seen before.

"He asked me to go steady on Christmas Eve. I always had to remember to hide the ring from my father." Her voice dropped and she closed her hand.

"Why?"

"My father didn't like Rob, didn't really want me to

see him, but especially not exclusively. I was all my father had. He was protective."

I was beginning to understand Constance a little better. I was all she had, too. Protecting me was what she thought she needed to do. I smiled at the thought of her putting herself between Mike and me when he had come to the house. She'd been like a mother cat protecting her kitten.

She reached into the box again and pulled out a pile of letters tied in a faded pink ribbon. She smiled at me. "If you don't mind I think I'll keep these to myself. Your father wrote me whenever we were apart. For a while, that is." The smile faded.

"This last thing might be the most interesting thing to you." I leaned over to see what she pulled out next. It was the same bumper sticker I had seen on the old rusty station wagon in the Sutton garage. GRACE HAPPENS spelled out in blue and yellow letters.

"I saw this today at the Suttons', but I don't get it." Constance handed it to me and I put it flat on the table and traced the letters with my finger.

"Your father designed this bumper sticker. It was part of a contest at school to come up with something that could be sold as a senior class fund-raiser. What nobody knew was that in some of our most serious talks we planned what our lives might be like someday. We even talked about what we would name our children. I loved the name Grace and your father used that in his design. It was our little secret." I looked up from the table to see Constance blushing.

"And you followed through; you named me Grace. I like that."

25. henry I

it had been a long day and I slept like the dead in my princess room, surrounded by lacy pillows and hugging Froggy.

When I opened my eyes, the sun was streaming through the window. The bedside clock registered 9:30. I stretched luxuriously under the covers before the events of the previous day came racing back. I ran my fingers through my hair and swung my feet over the side of the bed. When I stood up the loose board shifted under me. Constance had promised that everything would become clear today. My clothes from the day before lay in a heap on the floor in front of the closet door. The flannel boxers and tank I had worn to bed would be fine for grabbing breakfast. I could dress later. The house was silent and the door to Constance's room was closed. I tiptoed downstairs and pushed open the kitchen door.

A man leaned against the kitchen counter. "Hello, Grace." His voice was deep but hoarse. The long, dirty blond hair that hung almost to his shoulders was exactly the same color as mine. His jeans rode low on his hips and his black T-shirt looked faded from too much washing. Unlike Constance, every second of his age showed in his face. I guessed that our blue eyes weren't all we had in common as I hitched up my boxers and eyed his faded garb one more time.

I found my voice, but it came out soft and scared rather than large and in charge, the way I meant it. "What are you doing here so early?" I had expected our first meeting to be full of emotion. I had fantasized having the upper hand as the wronged child while he, the absent father, showered me with presents and fell to his knees apologizing for his absence in my life. Finding him in the kitchen dressed in jeans and a T-shirt was so ordinary, like he was there every day, just waiting to pour me a bowl of Count Chocula or chef me up his special eggs. But wasn't that what I thought I wanted? Ordinary?

"Your mother sent for me, Grace."

"I know, but she said she would be here."

"I'm a little early. I had trouble sleeping last night."

My father's blue eyes were bloodshot, but they were

unmistakably the Sutton eyes. "I don't know what to call you. Is it Henry L or Rob? I don't think Dad is an option."

My knees threatened to buckle, so I pulled out a chair and sat down. I didn't want him to realize the effect this meeting was having on me.

"You know my stage name. Are you a Flying Horses fan?" He smiled but it didn't cover the tension in his face. Maybe he was just as uncomfortable as I was.

"I prefer the Stones, but I know some of your stuff. Where's Constance?"

The box still sat on the table. I pulled it to me and rocked it back and forth. *Thud, thud, swish.* This is what I had waited for, what I had wanted, and now I didn't know how to handle it.

"So, Grace, your mother thought it was time we met."

I looked up. Anger pulsed through my every fiber. "Gee, ya think?"

"Look, Grace, there's a lot you don't know and I think it's time you heard the truth. At least the truth that I know. Connie may disagree with some of the finer points."

The door behind me scraped open. "That wouldn't be anything new, would it, Rob?" Constance's voice cut through the kitchen. "I thought we agreed on eleven o'clock. Grace, I'm sorry. I didn't realize anyone was here until I heard voices."

I turned my anger on her full throttle. "This is how

you clear things up for me? I never meet my father and you plant him in the kitchen one morning like a scene from a bad soap opera? I'm not an extra in one of your movies. I'm your daughter and I deserve better than this, Mother."

26. painted faces
tell no lies

The tears pressed against my eyes, but I fought them. I would not give these people, my parents, the satisfaction of seeing me cry. So, there we were: Constance Meredith, star; Rob Sutton, aka Henry L, lead singer and founder of the world-famous rock band Flying Horses; and me, Grace, named after a bumper sticker. I sniffed hard, wiped the back of my hand across my eyes, and said, "OK, I'm listening. Let's hear it."

Their story was pretty typical at first. Almost saccharine sweet. "Your mother didn't come to the island until our junior year in high school, and the first time I saw her at school I fell in love. At first she wouldn't have anything to do with me, but then came the first dance of the year. The band I was in then was playing."

Apparently, Rob Sutton did a horrible John Lennon

imitation that swept Connie Magurski off her three-inch platforms.

"After that we were inseparable," said Constance. "We even played the leads in the school production of *Grease* that year. The biggest problem was that my father didn't like him. Told me I could do better than a lead singer in a garage band, but I was in love and I had faith that he'd make it big someday." Constance had calmed down some and the edge had left her voice. She looked at her hands, turning them palm-up and then palm-down as she spoke.

Fast-forward to senior prom.

"We had made plans to take off after graduation," said Rob. "The band and I wanted to get off the island and see if we could land a record deal. Lots of new groups were making their first albums then and we thought we had a chance. I couldn't leave without Connie but somehow her father found out about our plans."

Constance sighed and gave me a thin smile. "My father came to the prom. He was livid. He pulled us apart in front of everyone and forbade your father to see me ever again."

"Connie tried to fight him, but he had a temper and I didn't want her to get hurt. I walked away." My father left his spot by the counter and sat down opposite Constance at the table.

That was why Constance still had his ring.

"My father was bitter because of what had happened

between him and my mother. He wanted a stable life for me. He didn't see that happening if I married a musician."

"He was right," my father reached halfway across the table as if to take her hand and must have thought better of it. He withdrew his hand.

"Your father left Martha's Vineyard after graduation. He took the band with him and they started playing little clubs and bars all over New England. I knew because he sent me the letters you saw last night through you grandmother. She always liked me."

"The band picked up a following and suddenly we had a record deal and an agent who said we needed to choose a distinctive name and identity. We were all from Martha's Vineyard and so we agreed on Flying Horses."

I couldn't contain myself. "But, why the painted faces?"

"Well, it worked for KISS, right? The face paint and stage names gave us anonymity. Without the face paint we were free to walk around in public and no one knew who we were." My father tugged on the neck of his faded T-shirt as if it were strangling him. "When we came back here to take the picture for our first album, your mother and I set up a plan with the help of our agent. While all of the hoopla was happening at the carousel with the photo shoot, your mother just walked out the front door of this house and headed straight to the airport and our private plane. No one even noticed her."

Now, I've been around Hollywood long enough to know that fairy-tale endings only happen in the movies, and as they talked I waited for the other shoe to drop.

"Before I knew it I was pregnant with you and Flying Horses was scheduled for a world tour." Was that a crack I heard in Constance's voice?

"The rest gets pretty ugly. We should have told you long ago, but we were both protecting ourselves and our careers." My father's eyes, the Sutton eyes, looked almost steely as he continued. "The road is a complicated place. There are lots of temptations. I gave in to almost every one of them. Your mother had gotten a nice apartment in L.A. and I was paying the rent while she waited for you to arrive."

"But you never came back," I said flatly. My eyes met his and I swallowed hard around the lump in my throat.

"No, Grace, I never came back. I got carried away on the road. I started drinking, and in my family that's not a good thing. We don't handle it well."

I remembered that Louise had called Mike an alcoholic.

"I got deeper and deeper into the bottle. It got so bad I couldn't go onstage without something to drink. We cancelled concerts because I couldn't perform. The rest of the band was no better. The manager we had at the time must have realized how easy it would be to swindle a bunch of drunks, so he pocketed a lot of money. I didn't know your mother had been evicted from her apartment. I was always too busy to take her calls, or asleep or hungover. I went through rehab five times before it took. I'm lucky to be alive. By that time your mother had taken you and walked away. She did the right thing, Grace. I was toxic. I wouldn't have been any kind of father to you."

"But how did you keep this all secret? It's impossible," I said.

My mother's face went pale, but she cleared her throat and the saga continued. "Grace, we were never married. We always meant to get around to it but we just never did. There's nothing on paper to connect us. Only island gossip, and that died out with nothing to fuel it."

"But your father must have known." I kept pushing, afraid that if I didn't they would stop talking and I would never know the full truth.

"I never saw my father again until I received word from Mrs. Sutton that he was really sick and needed care. By then he didn't recognize me anymore. I made arrangements for him and for the care of the house. I was young, Grace, and in love. I couldn't forgive him for taking such a harsh stand. I hope you can be more forgiving toward me."

I turned to my father. "And your family knew. They even swore Tanya to secrecy. Why?"

"Because I support them, Grace. My brother fell on hard times a few years back and threatened to go to the press with the whole story. Your mother's career was just taking off and it would have been bad publicity for her to have been associated with me. I was in and out of rehab, but the albums were still selling and I had money coming in."

"That bastard!" Constance hissed. "He told me you refused to pay him—that you didn't care about me or Grace. He threatened me with the press, too. I've paid him every month since Grace was five years old! I cut you totally out of our lives. . . . I thought you didn't care because you had hurt me so badly before. I couldn't stand to go through that again." My mother lowered her head and sobbed silently.

I had been right. There was no fairy-tale ending here. Just a big dose of reality in life in the fast lane. I had to ask one more question. "So what's changed? Why is it OK now for people to know about you? I mean, Louise knows, and by now her mother knows, and soon the whole island will know, so there goes Mike's little blackmailing scheme."

My father pulled on the neck of his T-shirt again. His Adam's apple bobbed up and down, and I wondered briefly if he was fighting tears like I was. At that moment I hoped so. "I have a proposition for you both," he said.

27. a normal life?

my life was not normal before I found my father, and it didn't get any more normal after he came into my life. After all, having Constance Meredith for a mother and Henry L for a father doesn't exactly make for an ordinary existence. So what if my father wears red leather pants, paints his face like a carousel horse, and goes onstage with a boa constrictor wrapped around his neck? That's his job.

His proposition was a good one. "Grace, I'd like to get to know you better if that's something you and your mother would like. My schedule is about to slow down, and it sounds like your mother's is speeding up. I have a house in Boston and one in L.A. How about if you come and spend a few weekends with me? I'm getting ready for a Flying Horses farewell concert. It's in Boston in a few weeks."

"What do you think, Grace?" My mother faced me and inclined her head in a half nod as if to say it was OK with her if I spent some time with my father. "Did I tell you we're shooting Vamp Two in Cambodia?"

"Boston is beginning to sound better and better, but I'd like to think it over." Since so many decisions had been made for me, this was one I wanted to consider. I felt exhausted, overloaded with information.

"Tell me about the concert," I said to my father.

"It's the last time we'll wear the face paint and the leather and travel with the snake. It's the last concert with fake blood and all the special effects. We've outgrown that stuff after sixteen years. We have an entire album of new songs written. Different stuff than we've ever done before." He grinned at me across the table in my mother's kitchen in the house on Martha's Vineyard. "The thing is, Grace, I'd like you to be there. If it's OK with your mother."

"Can I bring Louise?"

"I don't know her, but if she's your friend, absolutely," said my father.

An idea hit me right between the eyes then. I knew the perfect place to think everything through.

"I'm going to take a walk." I scraped back my chair, pushed open the kitchen door, rushed upstairs, and threw on my clothes from the day before. When I went out the front door, I could hear my parents still talking in the kitchen.

i spent the weekends leading up to the farewell concert with my father in Boston. Slowly, we were getting to know each other. He took me to all the tourist attractions and walked the busy streets as Rob Sutton. But the night of the concert was different. The limo delivered Louise, Toffee, Camilla, Constance, and me through a mob of screaming fans to the stage door. A huge security guard escorted us in and I was treated to a taste of Henry L's world.

"This is Henry L's dressing room." Our escort swung open the door, and there he was, Henry L, not Rob Sutton. That night, his long hair was spiked around his head with something that must have been like cement. His painted face was more garish than the carousel horse it was modeled after. The leather pants were black and laced up the front and legs. His boots had the highest platforms I had ever seen and his shirtsleeves were belled. In short, he looked awesome.

"Nice hair, Dad." It just slipped out. My face flamed. I waited for him to correct me and that's when I saw it. Push-pinned to the wall next to the mirror was a bumper sticker, faded and dog-eared, but still legible: GRACE HAPPENS.

My father must have seen me looking. "My mother sent me that when you were born. She knew that was where your mother and I got your name. Even in my lowest times I've kept that with me." He turned his attention to the rest of our little group. "I'm so glad you all came. His eyes rested a moment longer on my mother than anyone else. "Bruno will show you to the VIP section."

Louise seemed to be in shock. For once her smart mouth failed her. She followed Bruno mutely. Fifteen minutes later Flying Horses stepped onto the stage. The house lights went down and the roar was deafening. The audience rose to its feet and chanted and clapped. The band launched into one of its most famous songs.

"Hello, Boston!" My father's voice echoed over the sound system. "This is the Flying Horses farewell concert. We're going to sing all your old favorites, but we're going to do some new stuff, too, like this one. It's for a very special lady, and it's called 'Connie.'"

The first chords of a ballad rang out. Constance flipped her hair and tried to look in control, but I saw her wipe the corner of her eye. The crowd was restless. They expected hard rock from Flying Horses. What was this ballad junk? About halfway through, things quieted down.

Even rock fans know a good love song when they hear it.